He wanted to brand her, possess her, make her irrevocably his.

His heart thundered in his ears, and his blood pounded through his veins. He tore his mouth from hers, lowering his lips to the sweet hollow of her throat. "Allison, oh, Allison, I want you."

She stiffened, and Kent went rigid. Suddenly the past rose up to haunt him. All the times they'd kissed and touched. All the times she'd pulled away just when he wanted her most.

She was pulling away again.

He'd been fooling himself. Allison hadn't changed. She would never change. And once more she would send him out into the night.

Then, so softly he almost didn't hear it, came the whisper, "Oh, Kent . . . I want you, too."

Dear Reader,

Welcome to Silhouette **Special Edition** ... welcome to romance.

Last year, I requested your opinions on the books that we publish. Thank you for the many thoughtful comments. For the next few months, I'd like to share quotes with you from those letters. This seems very appropriate while we are in the midst of the THAT SPECIAL WOMAN! promotion. Each one of our readers is a **special** woman, as heroic as the heroines in our books.

Our THAT SPECIAL WOMAN! title for October is *On Her Own* by Pat Warren. This is a heroine to cheer for as she returns to her hometown and the man she never forgot.

Also in store for you in October is *Marriage Wanted,* the third book in Debbie Macomber's heartwarming trilogy, FROM THIS DAY FORWARD. And don't miss *Here Comes the Groom* by Trisha Alexander, a spin-off from her *Mother of the Groom.*

Rounding out the month are books from Marie Ferrarella, Elizabeth Bevarly and Elyn Day, who makes her Silhouette Debut as Special Edition's PREMIERE author.

I hope you enjoy this book, and all of the stories to come!

Sincerely,

Tara Gavin
Senior Editor

QUOTE OF THE MONTH:

''I'm the mother of six, grandmother of ten and a registered nurse. I work in a hospice facility and deal with death and dying forty hours a week. Romance novels, light and airy, are my release from the stress.''

L. O'Donnell
Maine

TRISHA ALEXANDER

HERE COMES THE GROOM

Silhouette®

SPECIAL EDITION®

Published by Silhouette Books New York
America's Publisher of Contemporary Romance

This book is dedicated to Loretta Kenny, the kind of friend every woman needs, and to the West Houston Chapter of the Romance Writers of America for their unwavering support over the years.

Special thanks to Marilyn Amann, Carla Luan, Heather MacAllister, Alaina Richardson and Sue Royer—critique group extraordinaire.

SILHOUETTE BOOKS
300 East 42nd St., New York, N.Y. 10017

HERE COMES THE GROOM

Copyright © 1993 by Patricia A. Kay

ISBN: 0-373-09845-6

First Silhouette Books printing October 1993

TRISHA ALEXANDER

has had a lifelong love-affair with books and always wanted to be a writer. She also loves cats, movies, the ocean, music, Broadway shows, cooking, traveling, being with her family and friends, Cajun food, *Calvin and Hobbes* and getting mail. Trisha and her husband have three grown children and one grandchild and live in Houston, Texas. Trisha loves to hear from readers. You can write to her in care of Silhouette.

Prologue

It is too late to call back yesterday...
Ancient Proverb

Allison Fornier tightened her arms around her two-month-old daughter. "Sleep, *mon bébé*," she whispered. "Don't be afraid. Soon we'll be home, and the doctors there will make you well. You'll see."

Marianne's tiny mouth tipped at the edges, as if she were smiling at her mother's words, and Allison's heart squeezed painfully. She cuddled the baby closer and stared blindly out the window of the Concorde jet as she blinked back tears.

There would be no more crying for Allison. She had already done her crying, and the crying hadn't solved anything.

Sighing deeply, she turned her gaze back to Marianne. Anyone giving the baby more than just a casual glance would realize something was wrong. There was a bluish cast to her nail beds and lips, and her skin color was dusky instead of creamy. These outward signs were an indication of serious problems involving Marianne's tiny little heart—a heart that didn't seem to work the way it should.

Allison still shivered every time she remembered Dr. Montand's solemn dark eyes, his grave tone of voice when he had delivered Marianne's sentence the day after her birth: "I am very sorry, Madame Fornier, but your daughter has a condition known as pulmonary atresia. Her body is compensating with collateral circulation to the lungs, but her pulmonary artery is too small, and not all the blood is being oxygenated as it should be."

Allison's throat had gone dry, and her heart had seemed to stop. "H-how serious is it, Doctor?"

"Very serious, I'm afraid. But we can correct the problem. It will require open-heart surgery, however." His eyes, liquid with compassion, had held her gaze.

"Open-heart surgery!" Just the thought scared Allison half to death. Marianne was so tiny. Open-heart surgery was so serious.

At first Allison hadn't wanted to believe Dr. Montand. How could this be possible? How could Marianne, so perfect, so beautiful, be in such danger? It couldn't be true. Dr. Montand *had* to be wrong.

But Dr. Montand hadn't been wrong. Dr. Deauville, the heart specialist who was brought in to oversee Marianne's tests, confirmed Dr. Montand's diagnosis. "Although we probably won't want to do the actual surgery until your daughter is a little older, we will monitor her carefully, *Madame*. If she shows signs of any deterioration at all, we may *have* to do the surgery.

But first we would do a heart catheterization. This would show us how much blockage there is." His voice had softened. "I realize all of this has been a great shock to you, *Madame*. Think about what I've said, and if you have any questions, please feel free to call me."

Before he left the room, he had added slowly, "I was very sorry to learn of your husband's death. All of France will miss him."

After he was gone, Allison remembered the doctor's words. If he only knew how guilty his words of sympathy had made her feel. He, like everyone else, thought she was devastated by the death of Jean Luc Fornier, her dashing race-car-driver husband, who had died in a crash seven months earlier, when she was two months pregnant with Marianne. The truth was, Allison mostly felt relieved that she no longer had to keep up the pretense of a happy marriage.

But Marianne. Marianne was different. Although Allison could barely tolerate Jean Luc toward the end of their marriage, she desperately loved her daughter and would have gladly laid down her life for her. Panic filled her at the thought that Marianne was so seriously ill.

For six weeks after she brought Marianne home from the hospital, all had gone well. Then one day Marianne's color had worsened, and Dr. Deauville confirmed Allison's fears.

"It's time to do the heart catheterization," he had said.

Fear had clogged Allison's throat. "But she's so little," she'd whispered. *And I'm so alone here.* "I—I'd like to call my father."

"Of course," Dr. Deauville had said. "We don't have to do the test immediately, but we shouldn't wait too long."

As the taxi sped Allison home to her apartment, she had done some hard thinking. She'd decided she didn't want to have the catheterization performed in Paris. She wasn't sure when her feelings about the city had changed. All she knew was that she no longer felt at home in Paris. She was afraid that from then on the city would always be associated with disaster in her mind. It was here that her marriage to Jean Luc had started to fall apart. It was here that she had received the news of his death. And it was here that the doctors had delivered their edict about Marianne.

After a long night of soul-searching, she had realized that what she wanted was to go home to Houston, no matter what she had to face when she got there. She had finally admitted she needed the comfort and security that only people who loved her could give her.

In the short time since she'd found out about Marianne's heart condition, she'd also discovered that many of the latest techniques concerning open-heart surgery had been perfected in France, but Houston also had world-renowned medical facilities, including top children's hospitals.

So, after conferring with the French doctors, she had decided she would take Marianne home—to the Children's Clinic of Houston. And the doctors there would cure her.

That decision had been made a week ago. Even though she had worked almost every available hour, it had still taken the better part of six days to get everything ready to leave. Packing, closing the apartment, storing the most valuable of the furniture and antiques, conferring with Jean Luc's attorney and banker, obtaining all the necessary records from Marianne's doctors—all took time and energy.

Madame Bergeron, the starchy housekeeper who had been with Jean Luc and Allison from the very first days of their ill-fated marriage, had cried when Allison said goodbye.

"Madame," Allison had said gently. "It's not too late. We can still get a passport for you. I would be happy to have you with me."

"Non, Madame," the housekeeper had said, wiping her eyes with her apron. "As much as I love the little one, how can I leave my own grandchildren?" She had kissed Marianne's forehead. "But I thank you for asking me."

Saying goodbye to Jean Luc's mother had been just as painful, but in a different way. Genevieve Fornier had Alzheimer's disease and wasn't even aware that she was seeing her only grandchild, perhaps for the last time.

Finally everything had been taken care of, all obstacles overcome, and now here they were, on the Concorde jet, due to land at JFK airport in just under an hour. Allison wondered what her reception would be when she arrived in Houston.

She knew her father would be overjoyed to see her. She wasn't so sure about her father's wife.

Diana.

Allison still remembered the reserve in Diana's cool blue eyes when she and Allison's father had arrived in Paris for Jean Luc's funeral. Oh, Diana was too much a lady to say or do anything but the correct thing. She had put her arms around Allison and comforted her. She had seemed genuinely concerned for her well-being.

But Allison hadn't been fooled. She knew Diana would never forgive her for what she had done.

And could Allison really blame her stepmother for her feelings? Allison had been engaged to Kent Sorensen, Diana's son. But she had broken that engagement only days before their scheduled wedding and run away to Paris. A few days later, when the invited guests showed up for what they thought would be a wedding between Allison and Kent, they had instead witnessed the vows of Allison's father, Lee, and Kent's mother, Diana.

Allison sighed, remembering the chaos she'd caused. The heartbreak and misery.

Yes, Diana would be a very odd mother not to disapprove of Allison. Now that Allison herself had a child, she understood how fiercely protective mother love could be. She had a much greater understanding of Diana's feelings. One of the things she had resolved to do from the moment she'd decided to go back to Houston was to try very hard to build a good relationship with her stepmother.

Stepmother.

That meant Kent was now her stepbrother. Funny that this was the first time she'd ever thought of him that way.

She tested the word.

Stepbrother.

Would she ever feel an easy camaraderie with Kent? A brotherly sisterly fondness?

No, she thought. Her feelings toward Kent were not sisterly. And she didn't think they ever would be.

Allison closed her eyes, memories of Kent flooding her mind. She could still picture him as he'd looked the night of their wedding-rehearsal dinner. She could still see the pain and unhappiness clouding his blue eyes, the shock and disbelief. She could still remember the look on his face when he'd realized she meant what she'd said, that she wasn't going to marry him after all.

She had been so wrong.

She knew that now.

She had thought of Kent often over the years. Thoughts of him had sustained her through many of the last miserable months. He was the one bright spot in an otherwise dark horizon. At least she knew that by releasing him from their engagement, she had allowed him to follow his dreams.

And as she gazed out the window at the mounds of white clouds below, looking for all the world like drifts of snow, she hoped he was happy.

But most of all, she hoped he had forgiven her.

Chapter One

Allison adjusted the slats of the miniblinds so she could see the backyard deck while no one outdoors would be able to see her.

Even though her stomach was jumping with nerves, she couldn't help smiling when she spied her father. Who would have thought that Lee Gabriel—sophisticated, urbane Lee Gabriel—could ever be so happily entrenched in suburban living?

Today her father, who was fast approaching his fifty-first birthday—a fact that still amazed Allison—was decked out in a silly apron and a tall chef's hat. As she watched, he bent over the big gas barbecue grill, doing something to the ribs he and Diana would be feeding their guests today.

While he worked, her stepmother walked into view. Diana set a big bowl of something on the picnic table, then headed for Lee. As she came up behind him, she reached out and patted his rear end.

Lee turned and laughingly caught his wife in his arms. Although Allison couldn't hear them, she could see Diana laughing, too, as she tried to escape Lee's hands, which slid down her back to caress her own rounded bottom. She lifted her face, and Lee gave her a long, lingering kiss.

Just the way her handsome father and his lovely blond wife stood—so close together that their bodies seemed molded into one—spoke volumes about the way they felt about each other. Although they'd been married more than three years, their body language said they still wanted each other with the intensity of newlyweds.

Allison stared, mesmerized, at the scene below. She knew she should look away. She knew this was a private moment, that Lee and Diana thought themselves unobserved. But she couldn't. She was like a starving woman, staring through a glass window at an array of freshly baked pastries that were beyond her reach.

Loneliness twisted through her. Loneliness and something else. A deep yearning.

What must it be like to be loved so well? To feel so comfortable with your love that you could show it with such unabashed joy and desire?

You could have had that, too. You threw it away.

She let the blinds fall back together. Stop it, she told herself. Stop feeling sorry for yourself. Count your blessings. And like a litany, she did.

She was healthy.

She was young.

She had a family who loved her.

And she had Marianne.

Beautiful Marianne, who was now napping in the nursery down the hall, a fact confirmed by the sound of her even breathing coming from the baby-room monitor Allison carried everywhere with her.

Marianne, who in a few short days would be entering the Children's Clinic of Houston for her heart catheterization.

Marianne, who Allison would not, could not, lose.

Remembering her baby daughter, Allison shook off her spurt of unhappiness over the past. There was no sense in spending even one moment of emotional energy on regrets. In the weeks and months to come, she would need every bit of her strength to help her deal with Marianne's medical problems.

Pull yourself together. Put on a cheerful face, go downstairs and help your father and his wife get ready to greet their guests, she scolded herself.

But even as she reminded herself what she knew she must do, she couldn't get rid of the butterflies fluttering around in her stomach. The butterflies caused by the knowledge that Kent had been invited to the Fourth of July celebration that would begin in minutes.

Would he come?

And if he did come, how would he act? Would he be happy to see her again? Or would he be cold and aloof? Maybe even angry?

Maybe he doesn't care at all. Maybe he no longer thinks I'm important enough to care about.

That thought hurt.

It hurt a lot, even though Allison knew she deserved whatever Kent wanted to dish out. When she'd first run away to Paris, she'd told herself Kent hadn't played fair with her. He'd led her to believe he was going to accept the associate law position with Keating & Shaw. Then, in the middle of their rehearsal dinner, he'd sprung the shocking news that he had changed his mind. He wasn't going to take the job and ensure their financial future. Instead, he planned to go ahead with his idealistic dream and open a storefront law office.

During the miserable weeks that followed, Allison told herself Kent was just as much at fault in their breakup as she was. And she even believed it.

But during her short-lived, disastrous marriage to Jean Luc, she quickly discovered it didn't matter how financially secure you were if there were no love and commitment to go along with it. It was only then that she had finally faced the truth.

She had traded substance for flash, gold for a cheap imitation, something solid for something that crumbled when you touched it.

She had done this.

She alone.

No one else.

She had lost Kent, tossed him away, and he had every right to despise her.

But even as Allison told herself these hard truths, she prayed he didn't really despise her. Maybe she could never have his love again, but she hoped, she prayed she could win his friendship. She needed a friend. She would know how hard a job that would be by this first meeting. She hoped she could get through it without falling apart.

As she had several times already, she wondered if Diana had purposely arranged for her and Kent to meet for the first time surrounded by a lot of people. After all, Diana was a kind woman. She would know how awkward and ill at ease both Kent and Allison would feel when facing each other for the first time since their breakup. She would want to try to smooth the way if she could.

Well, it was time to stop stalling. Allison picked up the baby monitor and started toward the door, then turned to take one more look at herself in the full-length mirror. She was dressed casually in army green walking shorts and a matching jungle-print blouse. As she smoothed her hair and stared at herself in the mirror, she wondered what Kent would see when he looked at her. She wondered if he would notice the changes that had taken place over the past years. She had taken great care with her makeup, wanting to hide the telltale smudges under her eyes—the smudges that advertised how little sleep she'd been getting lately.

Allison didn't want anyone, especially Kent, to feel sorry for her. Satisfied that she looked as good as she could, given the circumstances, she tiptoed into the adjoining room, took one last peek at Marianne, who slept soundly, then headed for the backyard.

Kent downshifted and impatiently tapped his fingers against the steering wheel of his white Corvette in time to Michael Bolton's rendition of "When a Man Loves a Woman." He eyed the car in the lane next to him—a Jeep filled with laughing girls clad in bathing suits and skimpy shorts. One of them, a beautiful dark-haired girl with come-hither brown eyes, winked at him.

Kent smiled cynically. Yep. They were all alike. The Corvette did it every time. Like Allison, money turned them on.

Allison.

His jaw tightened. Until yesterday he hadn't been sure he would even go to the Fourth of July party his mother and stepfather were hosting. Then, defiantly, telling himself not to be a coward, he'd invited Christina Sargent—another lawyer with his firm and someone he'd been dating for a while—to go to the party with him.

Normally Kent enjoyed spending time with Lee and his mother, but that had been spoiled now that Allison was back in Houston and living with them. Now he wouldn't be able to drop in for a cup of coffee or a beer. Now he would no longer feel relaxed and comfortable in their home.

Even his mother realized that everything had changed.

"You'll come to the party, won't you, Kent?" she'd asked, and he had heard the underlying tension in her voice.

"I don't know."

"You've got to get this meeting over with sometime."

"Yeah, I know."

"She's having a tough time right now, Kent. And she's a part of our family—like it or not."

"Yes, I guess you're right." How could he argue with the truth of his mother's statement? He was sorry that Allison's husband was dead and that her baby was sick. Of course he was. He wasn't insensitive or vindictive. Just because she'd discarded him like yesterday's garbage didn't mean he wished her bad luck. But he couldn't pretend he was happy to be forced into a family harmony that wouldn't exist as long as she was around.

Like it or not, his mother had said.

Well, he would never like it. As far as he was concerned, Allison Gabriel Fornier could have stayed on the other side of the world forever.

He wondered what his mother thought about all of this. That telephone conversation, which had taken place two days ago, had been the first time Diana had ever made a reference to the situation between him and Allison since Allison's hurried flight to Paris three and a half years earlier. Diana and Lee had gotten married at the ceremony that was intended to be Kent's and Allison's, shocking all of their friends and family with the unexpected turn of events.

Kent couldn't help grinning as he remembered that crazy day. Although he'd been in a state of near-paralysis over Allison's desertion, he'd still been happy for his mother. The press had had a field day, writing about the Sorensen-Gabriel wedding. They'd chortled over how the Sorensen turned out to be Diana instead of Kent, and the Gabriel turned out to be Lee instead of Allison. For days afterward there had been speculation over what had happened to cause the abrupt change, but Kent's family and friends had rallied around him and no one talked.

Kent knew they talked among themselves, though. But everyone, including his mother, seemed to understand that he couldn't talk about it. Couldn't talk about Allison. Not if he wanted to keep his emotions under control. Not if he wanted to heal.

So Diana carefully avoided the topic. Oh, she'd casually mentioned Allison's wedding to that big-shot Grand Prix race-car driver, Jean Luc Fornier, but she'd had to. She knew their marriage would be splashed all over the papers. And occasionally, but always in Lee's company, Diana would drop news of Allison in the conversation, so Kent was kept up-to-date on what was going on in Allison's life.

But she'd never alluded to their former relationship. Once Allison was gone and the wedding was off, Diana acted as if Kent no longer cared.

Kent had tried hard to foster that impression with everyone. It was different now, naturally, but for the first few months it had been very difficult to pretend indifference. Then, as the months passed, it got easier. But when Allison married Jean Luc, only four months after running out on Kent, Kent had had another bad spell. He'd lain awake many nights envisioning her with Jean Luc. Envisioning them making love. The fact that Jean Luc was famous, that his handsome, dark face had routinely been plastered all over the national magazines and newspapers so that Kent could easily picture them together, made the whole situation all the worse.

For a long time there had been an awful ache way down in his gut. He kept remembering how Allison had never let him make love to her. All during their engagement, she had insisted they wait until their wedding night. At the time he'd thought she just had high standards. That she wanted their wedding night to be special. That *she* was special. It had been tough, but he'd tamped down his passion. Now he realized what a fool he'd been. Allison had probably been withholding sex because he had refused to do what she wanted him to do.

Kent told himself he didn't care.

He told himself he was much better off without Allison.

He told himself she had never loved him, that all she had wanted was money and prestige, and when she thought she wasn't going to get them, she'd taken off without a backward glance.

She was cold and hard-hearted. A calculating little witch. She had never loved him at all.

He ignored the relentless voice that said Allison had never made any secret of what kind of life she expected when the two of them married. She had never approved of his idea to open a storefront law office and work there exclusively, to spend his days serving the underprivileged of Houston. She'd told him his plan wasn't practical, that they could not live on love alone. And when her father had arranged for Kent to receive an offer from Keating & Shaw, one of Houston's most prestigious law firms, and had suggested that Kent could combine the two—work days for the law firm, and with several other young lawyers do the *pro bono* work part-time—Kent had even admitted the suggestion was a sensible compromise.

He was all set to accept the offer.

But the day before their rehearsal dinner, he got cold feet. For so long he'd dreamed of the storefront office. For so long he'd thought of himself as some kind of white knight. He just couldn't relinquish those dreams.

He couldn't compromise. With him it was all or nothing.

So Allison had broken their engagement, in front of their families and friends, in the most painful way, and then she'd fled to Paris.

And now she was back.

Resentment and anger welled into his chest. He clenched his jaw. Damn! Why did her baby have to be sick? Why did she have to come back to Houston? It wasn't as if he could avoid seeing her. After all, as his mother had pointed out, they were related. Her father and his mother were married, which made him and Allison—what? Stepsiblings?

Kent grimaced. That was almost funny. Allison was his stepsister.

He wondered if she was still as beautiful and as sexy as she had been.

Now why are you thinking about that? Who cares? As Kent turned into the driveway of Christina's town-house complex, he told himself he didn't care. It made no difference to him whether Allison was gorgeous or ugly, shapely or skinny, sexy or prim.

He didn't give a damn.

Allison Gabriel Fornier no longer had the ability to upset him in any way. He would go to the party today. He would pay a lot of attention to Christina, who was his date for the day, and he would be coolly friendly toward Allison, just as if she were a casual acquaintance.

He would show her—and everyone else—that she was no longer important to him.

Lee looked at his watch. It was almost noon. "They should start arriving soon, don't you think?"

Diana smiled at him. She had just carried a stack of earthenware plates outside and placed them on the picnic table. "I told everyone any time after noon."

Lee lifted the lid of the gas grill again. Boy, those ribs looked good. He turned them, then basted them with his homemade barbecue sauce. "I'm glad it's a nice day," he said. For some reason, the powers-that-be had smiled on them, and instead of its customary one-hundred-plus, the mercury was only expected to reach ninety-two degrees today. Even the humidity wasn't too bad, considering this was July in Houston.

"Would you like something to drink, honey?" Diana asked.

"What've you got?"

"Fresh limeade, cold beer and all kinds of soft drinks."

"I'll have a glass of the limeade." Lee accepted the glass, then sank down into one of the comfortable redwood chairs dotting the deck. He looked at Diana, who sat perched on the edge of one of the long benches flanking either side of the picnic table. She looked particularly beautiful today, he thought, in her dark blue bathing suit and matching long skirt, which showed her tall, lush figure to advantage. At forty-seven, Diana was a strikingly attractive woman with gorgeous eyes, a beautiful smile and sleek blond hair. If anything, she was even lovelier now than the first day he'd seen her almost four years ago. He grinned, thinking about that meeting. He had gone with Allison to celebrate her engagement to Kent Sorensen and to meet Kent Sorensen's mother. Little did he dream that he would be meeting his destiny.

As he studied her, Diana stared out at the pool, her forehead knitted in thought.

"Diana, love, quit worrying," Lee said. "It's going to be all right."

Now she fastened her clear blue gaze on his. She sighed. "I hope so."

"They're both adults. They can handle this."

She shrugged. "I know they're adults but... Oh, I don't know. I've never been convinced that Kent was over Allison, and Allison...well, she seems awfully fragile right now. I'm concerned about her, too."

Lee felt a quiet pleasure at her words. He knew Allison was not one of Diana's favorite people, even though, to her credit, she had never once said so, and he realized his wife had tried very hard to be fair to his daughter. "She'll be okay," he said with more assurance than he actually felt. He was concerned about Allison, too. "She may look fragile, but she's a strong woman. Besides, she's just worried about the baby."

"Honey, I know. We're all worried about the baby." She sighed again, staring out toward the pool. Beyond the covered deck, the kidney-shaped pool sparkled aquamarine in the brilliant sunshine. "I pray everything will be all right."

"Yes, me, too." The baby's test was scheduled for early Wednesday morning, just five days away.

Diana was silent for a few moments, then she said, "I'm not even sure Kent's going to show up today."

"He'll come. He'll be too curious about Allison to stay away."

Now her direct blue gaze met his again. "You're hoping they'll get back together again, aren't you?" she said quietly.

Diana never failed to surprise Lee. And here he'd thought his secret wish had been well hidden. "Would that bother you?"

Her gaze never wavered. "I don't know. She hurt him a lot." A hint of sadness darkened her eyes. "He's changed because of it."

Lee didn't know what to say, but he was saved from saying anything because just then he heard the first car pull into the driveway. Almost simultaneously the back door opened and Allison, looking much too thin and tired to suit Lee, walked outside.

They'd been talking about her. She could see it in their faces as they both turned to look at her.

"Is the baby asleep?" Diana asked, giving her a welcoming smile.

Allison nodded. She heard the clunk of a car door slamming shut, then footsteps. All three of them looked toward the back gate. Allison's heart thundered in her chest. She licked her lips.

The gate opened.

Allison sighed with relief as she realized she'd been given a reprieve. It wasn't Kent entering the back gate. It was Diana's sister Carol, followed by two of her children and her husband. For the next half hour, new arrivals kept the momentum going: Diana's mother; her other sister, Jackie, with her two children; Lee's secretary, Britta, and her handsome husband, Bengt; two of Lee's associates; a couple of agents from Diana's real-estate office; and then Sunny Garcia, Diana's best friend and the manager of her office.

"Allison, I was so sorry to hear about your husband," Sunny said.

"Thank you." Allison had always liked Sunny, a perky redhead with an infectious grin.

"Where's the baby?"

"She's sleeping right now."

"Oh..." Sunny's forehead creased in disappointment. "I wanted to see her."

"Oh, you will, Sunny," Diana interjected. "Allison will bring her down later. Marianne won't sleep more than an hour or two."

"So how does it feel to be a grandmother?" Sunny asked.

"It feels wonderful," Diana said. "Marianne is a heartbreaker."

Allison wanted to hug Diana. No matter how Diana felt about her, she obviously loved Marianne. Their gazes met, and Diana smiled. Just then there was the thumping sound of another car door opening and closing, then more footsteps walking up the drive. Both Diana and Allison turned toward the gate.

Allison forgot to breathe as Kent, preceded by a leggy blonde who was laughing up at him, walked through the gate. Allison knew the exact moment he saw her, for the smile slid off his face. Time stood still as they stared at each other. Allison's mouth was dry. She wanted to say something, but she couldn't. Then, taking the blonde's hand, Kent walked toward her.

"Hello, Allison," he said. He smiled, but the smile didn't reach his eyes. "It's been a long time."

"Hello, Kent." She struggled to keep her voice as casual as his had been. "It's good to see you."

"Thanks." His blue eyes, so like his mother's, glinted in the sunlight. "It's good to see you, too." He turned toward the blonde. "Christina, this is Allison Fornier, my stepsister. Allison, this is Christina Sargent."

The blonde's gaze darted to Kent as if what he'd said had surprised her. Then she recovered and smiled at Allison, giving her a quick, appraising look. Allison met the blonde's gray-eyed gaze as Kent's words thrummed in her mind. *Stepsister.*

"It's nice to meet you," Christina said. She extended her hand, and Allison shook it. Then, her gaze sliding back to Kent's, Christina said, "I had no idea you had a stepsister. You've never mentioned her."

"She's been living in Paris," Kent said, avoiding Allison's eyes.

To Allison's intense relief, Diana walked over.

"Hi, Mom." The warm smile he gave her was like a knife twisting in Allison's heart. The thing she had always loved most about Kent was his incredibly warm smile. He put his arm around Christina, and the knife twisted deeper. "This is Christina Sargent. Christina—my mother, Diana Gabriel."

"It's very nice to meet you," Diana said. "You work with Kent, don't you? I remember him mentioning your name."

"Yes," Christina answered.

For a brief moment Allison thought about how Christina hardly looked the type to work at a store-front law office, but she was too nervous about seeing Kent again to examine the thought more closely.

After a few moments of chitchat, Diana said, "Why don't I introduce Christina to everyone?" She led the blonde off, leaving Allison alone with Kent.

Awkwardly Allison and Kent faced each other again. Allison's heart was beating so hard she was sure everyone could hear it. A welter of emotions rushed through her as she studied Kent: happiness, pain, confusion, regret, tenderness, fear.

He looked wonderful—deeply tanned and very handsome in dark swimming trunks and a white knit shirt. He looked exactly the way she had always pictured him, yet there was something different about him.

She tried to decide what the difference was. His dark hair was shorter than she remembered it and more stylishly cut, but that wasn't it. He looked older, of course, not so much the fresh-faced all-American boy, but more mature and filled out than he had been. But that wasn't it, either.

"I'm sorry about your husband," he said.

Allison swallowed against the pain that had lodged in her throat. Her hands trembled, and she clasped them together. "Thank you," she managed to say.

Something flickered in his eyes, something she wished she could believe was understanding, but it was gone so fast she couldn't be sure. "I hear your baby's sick," he said awkwardly.

She nodded. "Yes."

"I was sorry to hear that."

"Thanks." Oh, God, she hadn't felt this awkward and stupid since she was twelve years old. She wondered if he felt half as unhinged as she did.

"You're thinner," he said, looking her over.

Suddenly Allison wished she hadn't worn shorts. "Yes, well..." Why couldn't she think of something intelligent to say? What was the matter with her? She forced her mouth into a smile. "You know what they say—a woman can never be too thin or too rich."

His gaze met hers again. Now it was filled with...what? Disgust? Allison cringed inside. Her feeble attempt at humor had been a mistake. A big mistake. She was sure he had interpreted her stupid remark as a dig at him—a reminder that once financial security had been more important to her than him.

"The storefront must be doing well," Allison said, desperate to change the direction of their conversation.

Kent frowned. "What do you mean?"

"Well...um...your mother said that Christina works with you, so I thought—"

He stared at her. "I no longer have the storefront. I sold it."

Allison could almost feel the color draining out of her face as shock rippled through her. "You no longer have the storefront...." she repeated slowly. "Wh-where *are* you working?"

For one long moment he didn't answer. Then, with an odd expression in his eyes, he said, "I'm an associate with Keating & Shaw."

Just then the gate opened again and Sunny's daughter, Nikki, followed by a pleasant-looking, stocky man, entered the backyard. "Kent! Hi!" Nikki walked straight over to where Allison and Kent were standing.

"Hi, Nik," he said.

Still stunned by Kent's revelation, Allison fought to regain control of herself while watching Kent hug Nikki, then kiss her cheek. He grinned down at her, keeping his arm around her shoulders. Envy pricked Allison's heart. He hadn't so much as touched *her* hand when he'd greeted her. Finally Nikki disengaged herself and turned to her.

"Allison! It's good to see you again!" she said, a big smile lighting her face.

"Hello, Nikki. It's good to see you, too."

With no hesitation at all, Nikki leaned forward and hugged Allison. The hug surprised Allison. God knows, they'd never been friends, and even though Allison was sure Nikki was happy about the breakup of Kent and Allison's engagement, she hadn't expected a warm welcome from Nikki. When two women loved the same man, it was impossible for them to be friends. And Nikki had loved Kent as much as Allison loved him. In fact, Allison wouldn't have been surprised if Nikki had shown up at today's party on Kent's arm.

"I'd like you to meet my husband, Glenn Prescott. Glenn, this is Allison Fornier." Nikki smiled proudly.

Allison hoped she'd disguised this second shock, for she had had no idea Nikki was married. Somehow she'd thought Nikki would always be in love with Kent.

"Nice to meet you," Glenn Prescott said, extending his hand.

He had a firm handshake and soft hazel eyes. He gave Allison a friendly smile, and she could feel herself responding.

They made small talk for a few minutes, then Nikki excused herself to go to talk to her mother. Glenn and Kent gravitated toward the rest of the men, who had congregated in a group and, if the bits of conversation Allison overheard meant anything, were discussing yesterday's Astros' game.

Allison walked over to the other end of the deck and sat on the railing. She wished she were anywhere but here. Trying to pretend this was just a normal holiday gathering, trying to pretend that there had never been anything between her and Kent, trying to pretend she was comfortable around him—all had her stomach in knots. Fingering the baby monitor, she wondered how soon she could escape, maybe say she had to go check on Marianne.

As the thought crossed her mind, Kent's clear laugh rang out, and the yearning Allison had felt earlier returned. It settled deep into her belly, throbbing with a dull ache.

At that moment Kent turned his head, and across the distance separating them, their gazes met and locked. Something hard and bright shimmered in the depths of his eyes, and just before he looked away, Allison realized what it was.

Hate.

He hated her.

Chapter Two

He wanted to hate her.

He had fully intended to hate her.

Instead, Kent's heart had twisted at the sight of her. Gone was the bright, assured, sassy woman he'd once known. In her place stood a woman who looked fragile and vulnerable. A bone-deep sadness haunted the depths of Allison's golden brown eyes. A sadness Kent wished he could ignore. A sadness that made her look older than her twenty-six years.

Inwardly he grimaced. Obviously the death of her husband had hit her hard. Kent realized that up until this moment, he'd harbored a secret hope that her marriage to the hotshot racer had been one of expediency instead of love. Now he knew it wasn't.

How could she fall in love so fast? So soon after breaking *their* engagement?

Because she never loved you at all, you idiot.

His jaw hardened as his gaze swept over her body. She'd lost too much weight. And he didn't think she'd done it on purpose, despite her flippant remark about no woman being too thin or too rich.

Even in the face of these changes, she was still beautiful. Covertly he studied her, cataloging the differences the years had made.

Her hair was shorter but still lustrous and thick, a rich dark brown streaked with gold. He'd always teased her about her hair and eyes being a matched pair.

Those eyes. Kent had dreamed about her eyes too many nights to count. Even sorrowful, they were captivating—sultry, thick lashed and a dreamy shade of topaz.

Same tip-tilted nose.

Same cleft chin, inherited from her father.

Same high cheekbones.

Same slightly exotic look.

His gaze dropped to her mouth. That mouth sure brought back some memories. Memories he'd rather forget. Full and lush, her lips invited a man's kiss.

Kent tried to push the thought away, but his mind kept returning to it. He kept remembering the kisses they'd shared. He could still taste her, the sweet, dark recesses of her mouth. The way his blood would pump when they kissed and touched. How much he'd loved her and wanted her.

And how she'd continually refused him.

Remembering, the pain he'd so successfully submerged had threatened to erupt again.

Damn, he thought. *She means nothing to me. Why am I dredging up all this ancient history?*

Even as he told himself all this, he couldn't look away. And he couldn't stop the memories.

She looked different, yet so familiar. They had been apart three and a half years, but the months they'd been together seemed like yesterday as they came rushing back. Images he'd once thought were long dead resurfaced.

Allison laughing up at him.

Allison looking so sexy and beautiful at their engagement party that Kent's mouth had gone dry every time he looked at her.

Allison, eyes bright with tears, at their rehearsal dinner, where she'd broken their engagement then disappeared from his life.

Jesus, she'd gotten under his skin. He'd loved her so much. And she had nearly killed him when she walked out on him.

Forget all that. It's over.

He tried not to look at her sitting by herself. But his gaze kept returning to her. He pretended to be engrossed in the men's discussion of last night's Astros' game, but his eyes and mind kept straying in her direction.

"Kent, are you going to stand here and talk sports all day?"

Kent turned at Christina's comment. She smiled at him, her gray eyes smoldering as they swept his face possessively. For the first time since he and Christina had begun dating, Kent felt a faint twinge of annoyance. "Sorry," he said, turning toward her. "Is there something you'd like to do?"

"Why don't we swim?" she suggested. "I wore my suit under this." As she spoke, she began to unbutton her red jumpsuit. When she stepped out of it, she was clad in a wispy black bikini that showed her tall figure to advantage. She smiled over her shoulder as she walked toward the pool. Kent watched her as he rid himself of his knit shirt and shoes.

Christina was, like him, an associate with Keating & Shaw, and a month ago they had both been assigned to a big case under Colin Jamieson, one of the senior partners. Because their role in the case involved extensive research, they had been thrown together a lot.

Kent had been attracted to Christina from the first. And she made no secret of her interest in him. So it had seemed natural that after a long day's work, they would go out for dinner together. And still more natural to end the evening at Kent's condo or Christina's town house.

Kent had enjoyed the time he'd spent with her. She was smart, beautiful and entertaining. She was also aggressive and had a sharp legal mind. She stimulated him, both personally and professionally.

Christina was, in fact, everything he could possibly want in a woman. At this very moment she was lying on her back in the glistening water, beckoning him with her lazy smile.

He wondered if Allison was watching.

He knew it was petty, but he wanted her to see that he had done very well for himself. That he hadn't been sitting around mooning over her.

He walked toward the pool, casting one last glance over his shoulder before diving in.

As the minutes passed, Allison wished desperately for a reason to leave the lively crowd. She felt miserably uncomfortable since seeing that cold expression in Kent's eyes. It had been bad enough before he'd arrived. Then she'd only wondered what his reaction to her would be.

Now she knew.

And knowing was infinitely worse than speculating.

She tried not to look at him again after that one revealing glare he'd given her. Yet she couldn't seem to keep her gaze or her thoughts away from him.

And when his date approached him and said something, and Kent smiled in response, something inside Allison had contorted painfully.

Once Kent had looked at her that way.

Once he had smiled at her that way.

Once his heart had belonged to her.

It was all she could do to keep sitting there, acting as if she didn't care what Kent did, pretending not to watch as Christina took off her red jumpsuit and walked seductively toward the pool.

Watching Kent watching Christina was like having someone stick a knife into her; the pain was just as sharp. And when he began to walk toward the pool to join the beautiful blonde, Allison could stand the torture no longer. She stood abruptly and walked toward the back door with the intention of going inside to check on Marianne, even though there were no sounds from the baby monitor.

"Allison, I'm dying to see your baby."

Allison turned at the sound of Nikki's voice. She smiled. "I was just going to go inside to check on her. Do you want to come?"

Nikki grinned. "You bet."

Allison studied her companion as they walked into the house together. Nikki Garcia Prescott, like Kent, had changed since Allison had last seen her. The changes were for the better. Her sleek dark hair was cut in an attractive pixie style that suited her small face, and she'd learned how to apply makeup and dress more attractively. She also acted more confidently than she had three and a half years ago. Allison wondered if marriage had given her that contented, self-assured air. "I was surprised to meet Glenn," Allison said. "No one told me you'd gotten married."

Nikki smiled happily. "We've only been married for eleven months."

"He seems awfully nice." Allison led the way upstairs. "How'd you meet him?"

"We work together."

By now they'd reached the baby's room, and Allison put her finger to her lips. "If she's still sleeping, I don't want to wake her," she whispered.

Nikki nodded.

Allison gently pushed the door open, and they tiptoed over to the crib. As they approached, Marianne stirred, and her eyelids fluttered open.

"Oh," Nikki said softly. "She's beautiful...."

Something constricted in Allison's chest as she gazed down at her baby. She wondered if she would ever look at Marianne without feeling awed that this exquisite creature belonged to her. She turned off the monitor, then leaned over the crib. "Hi, sweetie."

Marianne rewarded her with a smile, and Allison choked up. At two months Marianne had just begun smiling, and each time she did, Allison felt this same, almost embarrassing emotion. She'd had no idea she would love her baby so fiercely. Before she'd gotten married, she had occasionally thought about having children, but she hadn't realized how miraculous it would be. Now that she had her daughter, she couldn't imagine life without her.

She picked up the baby, holding her warm little body close for a second, inhaling the sweet baby smell.

"Oh, can I hold her?" Nikki asked, her eyes shining eagerly.

"Just let me change her first." Allison walked toward the changing table, and Nikki followed her.

"She's wonderful," Nikki said, shyly touching Marianne's head.

Allison took off Marianne's diaper and dropped it into the diaper pail. She reached for a fresh diaper. "She is, isn't she?"

"My—my mother told me about her heart." Nikki gently rubbed Marianne's head. "But she doesn't look sick."

"Except for her color." Allison believed in putting people at ease, so she tried to be matter-of-fact when she talked about Marianne's problems.

"Even her color isn't that noticeable."

"No. Not today. But sometimes it is." Allison deftly cleaned Marianne and put on the new diaper. "We have to keep her as quiet as possible."

Nikki nodded. "You know, Allison, I really admire you."

"Me?" Allison resnapped Marianne's knit outfit. "Whatever for?"

"You just seem so capable, and . . . well, you've survived everything so well."

"I guess I put up a good front." She lifted the baby and handed her to Nikki. "I have my bad days, believe me."

"Well, you've done the right thing coming home. I know Diana and Lee are happy you're closer." Nikki cuddled Marianne, and Marianne's big eyes fastened on Nikki's face.

"Some people aren't so happy," Allison muttered before she could stop herself. Oh, great. Why had she said that?

There was silence for a moment. Then Nikki asked, "Are you referring to Kent?"

Allison nodded.

"Well, it's really none of my business, but... Oh, shoot. It really is none of my business."

Allison grimaced. "No. Go ahead. Say whatever it is you were going to say."

Nikki shook her head.

"Come on, Nikki. I'm the one who brought up the subject. I can take it."

Nikki's green eyes were thoughtful as they studied her. "Well, you can't really blame Kent if he still harbors some bitterness toward you."

"No, you're right."

"You hurt him a lot," Nikki said, her voice soft.

"I know." Allison sighed deeply. "It's funny. After I went to Paris, I fully expected Diana to write me and say Kent had married *you.*"

Nikki's gaze met hers again. "I guess for a while I hoped that would happen, too. But it wasn't meant to be. He was never in love with me, and he never will be." Then she smiled, her eyes softening with happiness. "And now, of course, I'm so glad because I met Glenn, and he's wonderful."

Allison returned her smile. "You're lucky." *I wasn't so lucky, but that's my own fault.*

A few minutes later Allison heated a bottle for Marianne while Nikki held her and cooed to her. Marianne, who usually complained loudly when it was time for her feeding, seemed mesmerized by Nikki's soft drawl and kept rewarding her with smiles.

"Her eyes are beautiful," Nikki said. "Wonder if they'll stay blue?"

"I don't know. Her father had blue eyes, so they may." One of the reasons Allison had been attracted to Jean Luc initially was because his eyes had reminded her of Kent's. She knew that now. She hadn't known it at the time.

"You must miss him a lot."

Allison shrugged. She refused to lie and say she did. She was sorry Jean Luc was dead, because no man should die so young. She was sorry he'd never know his beautiful daughter. And she was sorry they'd made each other so unhappy.

But she didn't miss him.

When the bottle was ready, Allison took Marianne from Nikki. "I'm going to go sit in the rocking chair in the den and feed her."

"Oh, bring her outside! Everyone wants to see her."

"I'll bring her out when I'm through." Allison didn't feel like explaining that she always started out by breast-feeding Marianne and didn't want to do that in front of dozens of people. The bottle would just be supplementary because she didn't have enough milk to satisfy the baby.

"Promise?" Nikki said.

"Yes. I promise."

Kent wondered when Allison had left the party. One minute she was there, the next she wasn't. He swam toward the edge of the pool. He'd had enough of the water, he decided.

After climbing out, he toweled himself dry and reached for his knit shirt.

"The ribs are almost ready," Lee called from the grill. "Is anyone hungry?"

This question was met with a chorus of cheers and affirmative answers. Kent scanned the patio again, then headed for the cooler where the beer was stashed. Reaching down, he took out a can and popped the top. As he took a long swallow, he saw Nikki emerge from the back door of the house.

Smiling, he walked over to her. He didn't see enough of Nikki. They'd been best friends since their toddler days when Nikki's mother had baby-sat him while his mother attended real-estate school. And their friendship had only strengthened over the years. Nikki had been the sister he'd never had. All through their school years they'd done homework together, told each other their troubles and shared each other's triumphs.

Nikki had taught Kent how to dance.

And Kent had taught Nikki how to drive.

Rarely had a night gone by that they didn't talk on the phone.

It was only after Kent had started college at the University of Houston and Nikki went to work that they began to drift apart. Each made other friends. Somehow Nikki didn't seem to fit in with Kent's crowd, and he felt out of place with her cohorts from work.

Still, their friendship was the kind that when they did see each other, there was never any awkwardness between them.

No, Kent thought. The awkwardness had begun about five years ago when Kent was twenty-three and Nikki was twenty-two. That's when her feelings toward him had changed. Instead of friendship, she had fallen in love with him, and Kent had not felt the same way. He had loved her, but he hadn't been in love with her.

When he met Allison and fell in love with her, that had really put a strain on his relationship with Nikki, for Allison hadn't liked Nikki, and that dislike was obvious. He'd never been sure how Nikki felt about Allison. She'd acted as if she liked her, but maybe that was strictly for his sake. Funny, he thought, that he'd never asked her.

Now, though, things had come full circle. Allison and Kent had broken their engagement, and Allison had left Houston. Nikki had met Glenn and gotten married and was obviously very happy. Nikki and Kent were once more best friends. And now Allison had reentered their lives.

"So, I haven't seen you for a while," he said as he reached Nikki's side. "What've you and Glenn been doing?"

She smiled up at him. "Can I tell you a secret?" Her green eyes, one of her prettiest features, Kent thought, sparkled.

"Sure. You know you can."

"Glenn and I are expecting a baby." Her eyes glowed with happiness.

"Gee, Nik, that's great!" Kent felt a sudden twinge of envy, which he quickly forced away.

"Yes, we're absolutely thrilled. But don't say anything, okay? It's too early to tell people, but, well, you're like a brother to me, so I had to tell you."

Kent hugged her.

"Should I be jealous?" asked a male voice behind Kent.

Kent turned. Nikki's husband, Glenn, stood there, a big smile on his face. "I'm the one who's jealous. Your wife just told me your great news."

Glenn beamed and slipped his arm around Nikki. "Yeah, we're pretty happy."

"Oh, honey, I just saw Allison's baby," Nikki said, "and she's so beautiful!" Her sparkling gaze met Kent's. "Don't you think so, Kent?"

"I haven't seen her yet."

"You haven't?" She gave Kent an odd look.

He kept his face carefully blank. "Nope."

"Well, you'll get your chance soon. Allison said she'd bring the baby outside after she finishes feeding her."

Kent nonchalantly looked toward the house. The back door remained closed.

"So, Kent, who's your date?" Nikki asked.

"Christina? We work together." He avoided her gaze. She was altogether too damned perceptive.

"She's a lawyer?"

"Uh-huh. We're assigned to the same case right now."

"Have you been dating her long?"

"For about six weeks, I guess."

"Is it serious?"

"Boy, you're nosy," he said, grinning at Glenn, who stood quietly smiling.

"She is, isn't she?" Glenn said, giving Kent a conspiratorial wink.

Nikki playfully punched Glenn on the arm. "Come on, Kent. Don't be mean. I just want everyone to be as happy as we are."

"You mean you just want to see everyone married," Glenn said.

"Oh, give me a break," she said, laughing. Then she turned to Kent again. "Well, is it?"

"Is it what?" Kent teased.

"Kent!"

"No, it's not serious," he said, relenting.

"Christina sure is great looking," Glenn said.

"Now wait a minute..." Nikki said. "You're married, remember?"

"Maybe married, but not dead," Glenn retorted. Then he looked over Kent's shoulder. "Speaking of your date, here she comes now."

Kent turned around. Christina was headed their way. She still wore her bathing suit, but she'd wrapped a blue beach towel around her body, sarong style. Kent noticed how several of the men ogled her as she walked by. She smiled as she reached them. "Don't you want to get something to eat?" she asked Kent.

Just as Kent started to answer, the back door opened, and Allison, carrying her baby, walked out. Nikki turned. Within minutes Allison was surrounded by people exclaiming over the baby. Nikki and Glenn drifted away, and Kent and Christina were left by themselves.

"I still can't get over the fact that you've got a stepsister and never told me," Christina said, her eyes on Allison.

Kent kept his voice light. "There are probably lots of things I haven't told you."

"But I know we've talked about your family. You told me all about your mother. You even told me about Nikki. Why didn't you tell me about Allison?"

Kent shrugged. "Subject just never came up." He forced himself not to look in Allison's direction, but it was difficult because of all the excitement her appearance with her baby had generated.

Christina gave him an odd look. "Why do I get the feeling there's something more here than meets the eye?"

He frowned. "You're imagining things."

"Am I?"

"Yes." Because he wanted to change the subject, he suggested, "Why don't we get something to eat?"

Ten minutes later, plates laden with barbecued ribs, baked beans, coleslaw and rolls, they found a couple of empty lawn chairs and sat down.

Not long after, Lee walked over and sat down next to Christina. "I haven't had a chance to talk to you," he said to her. "I understand you work with Kent."

Christina smiled. "Yes."

"You must be a very good lawyer."

"I am."

Lee laughed. "I like that. No coy answer. No false humility."

She shrugged. "I don't believe in hiding my light under a bushel."

That was certainly true, Kent thought.

"Good for you," Lee said.

Kent smiled as he listened to the exchange. He admired and respected his stepfather. He had liked him from the first moment he'd met him. Of course, at the time he'd thought Lee was going to be his father-in-law. As he remembered that day, Kent's attention wandered from the conversation, and his thoughts once more drifted to Allison. Out of the corner of his eye, he could see her, flanked by his mother and Nikki's mother as she walked to the edge of the patio and sat in one of the redwood deck chairs.

"Well, enjoy your food," Lee said about ten minutes later as he got up and walked away.

They finished eating, Kent forcing himself to listen to Christina's chatter and not look in Allison's direction. Then, because he knew the longer he waited the more difficult it would be, he said, "I think I'll go over and meet my little stepniece."

"I'll go with you," Christina said, "although babies really aren't my bag."

Kent knew that. Christina had made this same remark several times in his hearing.

They walked over to where Allison was sitting just as Kent's mother stood up. She smiled at him, and he smiled back. Nikki's mother, Sunny, also stood, saying, "Well, it looks as if you've got some other people who want to see the baby. Here, Christina... it is Christina, isn't it?"

"Yes," Christina said.

"You can have my seat," Sunny continued.

"And you can have mine," Diana said to Kent.

Kent hadn't intended to sit down. He'd had some idea of walking up, giving the baby a quick once-over and walking away again. But he sat.

His gaze met Allison's. "This is Marianne," she said, her voice soft. Slowly he looked at the baby.

"Hi," he said, leaning closer.

Marianne's huge eyes turned toward him. She studied him gravely.

"Hi, there," he said again, feeling a little silly because he didn't know how to act.

Marianne smiled, waving her little fists in the air.

Kent's heart turned over. Mesmerized, he reached out to touch her hand, and she closed her tiny fingers around his thumb. The feel of warm baby was like no other he'd ever experienced.

"What do you think of her?" Allison asked.

Eyes still on Marianne, he said, "She's beautiful."

"How old is she?" Christina asked.

Kent had almost forgotten Christina was there.

"She's almost two months old," Allison replied, turning toward Christina.

Christina gave the baby a cursory look. "She's very pretty," she said. "Your father told me you were married to Jean Luc Fornier. I'm sorry about what happened to him."

Kent looked at Allison. She avoided his eyes. "Thank you," she said.

"I really gave Kent the business for not telling me you even existed. I still can't believe it. He has a stepsister married to a famous race-car driver, and he never even mentions it."

At that moment Kent wanted to strangle Christina. He was saved from having to say anything when Lee's secretary, Britta, walked up to them and began cooing over the baby.

"See you later, Allison," Kent said. Standing, he said to Christina, "You coming?" Without waiting for her, he walked straight toward the cooler.

By the time he'd opened a beer and taken a long swallow, he'd gotten control of his emotions.

"What's the deal between you and your stepsister?" Christina asked. "Is there bad blood between you?"

"Why do you ask that?" Kent said. Just to prove that he could, he met her gaze evenly.

"I don't know," Christina said slowly. "I just got a funny feeling while we were talking to her. It's as if you don't like her much."

"I like her fine."

Christina shrugged. "The two of you seem awfully stiff together."

Kent's jaw hardened. Damn it all. He didn't want to get into it, but he knew if he didn't tell Christina some of the background between him and Allison, she'd find out sometime, anyway. And then she'd attach even more importance to Kent's not telling her than she already had. Not only that, she'd think Allison still mattered to Kent. He took another swallow of beer. "Okay. I might as well tell you. Allison and I used to be engaged to each other." As he spoke, he met her gaze squarely.

Her jaw dropped. She didn't say a word for a moment, then her eyes narrowed. "And you didn't think it was important enough to tell me?"

Kent shrugged. "It's ancient history."

She stared at him. "What else haven't you told me?"

"I don't know why you're making such a big deal out of this," he countered. "We didn't have an amicable parting of ways, okay? So I'd rather not talk about it, okay? That's why I didn't tell you. Okay?"

"Fine," she said tightly.

Anyone looking at her would be able to tell she was angry. Suddenly Kent was ashamed of himself. Just because he still hadn't come to terms with his feelings for Allison didn't mean he should take it out on Christina. "Hey," he said softly, touching her shoulder. "I'm sorry. Maybe I should have told you, but like I said, Allison and I . . . well, things are awkward between us. I guess they always will be."

"Are you still in love with her, Kent?"

He looked into her cool gray eyes. "No."

"Are you sure? Because if you are, tell me now."

"I'm not. Allison and I are completely finished."

"I hope you're telling me the truth."

Defiantly, hoping Allison was watching, Kent bent down and gave Christina a lingering kiss. "Now do you believe me?" he asked when he lifted his head.

He ignored the small voice inside that asked, *hey, buddy, who are you trying to convince?*

Chapter Three

"Great game, Kent."

Kent zipped up the cover over his tennis racket and grimaced at Bobby Halloran, his old college roommate. "Maybe for you. But I sure have had better days."

Bobby laughed. "Well, if you're looking for sympathy from me, buddy, you're barking up the wrong tree. I've been on the losing end too often. It's about time I won a match!" He waved. "See you next week."

"Yeah."

Kent tossed his gear into his car, climbed in, started the engine and pointed the Corvette toward home. He couldn't wait to jump in the shower after his sweaty exercise in futility. As he drove, he thought about the game. He and Bobby had played tennis together early every Sunday morning since both were freshmen at the University of Houston. Normally Kent enjoyed their game. But it was hard to enjoy what had happened to him this morning. He'd missed easy returns, double-faulted several times during his serve and practically handed Bobby the match. For some reason, his concentration had been shot.

Who was he kidding, anyway? He knew damned well why he hadn't been able to concentrate today. Ever since the party at his mother's house on Friday—the party where he'd come face-to-face with his past—his mind had been on one thing and one thing only.

Allison.

He kept reliving the months of their engagement. Remembering all the things that had happened between them. Replaying old conversations. Rehashing old hurts. Wondering if there was anything he could have done differently.

God, he was sick of it. What was done was done. Why couldn't he leave it alone?

Because she came back, that's why. As long as she wasn't around, you could pretend none of it mattered. But now she's here, and you can't pretend anymore.

"I don't care about her," he muttered angrily. Someone behind him hit his car horn, and Kent jumped. He was stopped for a red light. The light had turned green, and he hadn't even known it. He jammed the car into gear and took off with a peal of rubber.

For the rest of the way home, he forced himself not to think about anything except what he would do for the remainder of the day. He usually spent some portion of the weekend with Christina, but she had gone to San Antonio to visit her parents this weekend. She'd invited him to come along, but he'd declined. Going to meet a woman's parents implied a serious relationship.

And Kent wasn't sure he was ready to have Christina *or* her parents make that assumption.

So what should he do now that he had a free day? He could go into the office. Lord knows, he always had plenty of work to do there. But he didn't feel like working today. He'd been doing too much of that lately, what with his new assignment and the firm's insistence on every associate billing a certain number of hours per week.

Kent frowned. Billable hours was one aspect of working at Keating & Shaw that still bothered him. He wondered if other firms engaged in the practice of padding. He'd been pretty naive when he was hired and had questioned Ben Keating's order to bill a minimum of sixty hours per week. When Kent had commented on the order to one of the other associates, saying he didn't see how anyone could work sixty-hour weeks every week, it had been explained to him that if he made a one-minute phone call, he was to bill a quarter hour, which was the smallest amount of billed time allowed. With that guideline, a lawyer could put in fifty actual hours but bill eighty.

For the past year and a half, Kent had obediently followed the firm's guidelines, just as every member of the firm did. Yet the practice continued to disturb him. Still, he said nothing because he wanted to keep his job. Eventually he hoped to make partner. If that meant he had to compromise, so be it. That was the way of the world, as he'd learned the hard way. Compromise. Negotiate. Make deals.

So he kept his mouth shut, his nose clean, and did what he was told. Let someone else be a squeaky wheel. Squeaky wheels did not make partner. Squeaky wheels either got fired or they got assigned to the most boring, routine cases and remained in their small, stuffy cubicles forever.

Kent wanted a corner office with a big window. And he wanted to work on exciting, career-making cases. No more playing at Don Quixote for him. His hard work and cooperative attitude were beginning to pay off, too. Several months ago he'd been assigned to a big personal-injury case involving one of Keating & Shaw's most important clients—Emmett Wilder. Suit had been brought against Wilder by Shelley Petrowski, the widow of Greg Petrowski, who had been killed while testing the Wild Rider, a motorcycle designed and manufactured by Wilder's company.

Kent had been thrilled to be assigned to work with Colin Jamieson, the senior partner in charge of the case. Kent knew that a case like this was the kind of assignment that made a new associate's career. Do a good job, impress Colin Jamieson and Kent would be on his way toward his partnership.

But despite his enthusiasm for the Wilder case, he still didn't feel like working today.

Well, if he didn't work, what should he do with the rest of his day? Catch up on his reading? Drop into Dusty's and watch the Astros' game with a bunch of the guys? Yeah, that sounded good. And on the way, he could stop at his mother's and leave the new wills he'd prepared for her and Lee at their request.

You don't have to do that, he reminded himself. Lee said he'd come by your office and pick them up. Are you looking for an excuse to see Allison again?

Kent ignored the taunting voice. Of course he wasn't looking for an excuse to see Allison again. Lee did so much for him that he simply wanted to save Lee some hassle.

Uh-huh. And the moon is made of green cheese.

Kent gritted his teeth. He'd be damned if he'd completely change his life just because Allison was now back in Houston. Why should he have to avoid his mother's house? Why should he have to do anything different from what he'd been doing?

He would take the wills over there, he thought defiantly. And if he did happen to see Allison, he would simply say "hi" and nothing else. He would continue to show her how little importance her existence held for him.

Because if he didn't go, if he let Allison's presence in his mother's home deter him from his normal routine or stop him from dropping in as he was accustomed to doing, then he would be giving her control of his life.

Allison decided she would put on her bathing suit and go lie in the sun for a while. Marianne had just gone to sleep for her afternoon nap, Diana had gone out for one of her rare weekend appointments to show houses to a client, and her father was working on his computer in the study.

Armed with the baby monitor, a book, sun block and a beach towel, Allison walked out to the pool. Head protected by a big straw hat, she donned her sunglasses, stretched out on a chaise lounge and opened her book.

About forty-five minutes later, she wondered if perhaps she'd had enough sun for one day. Maybe she should cover up or go inside. Just as the thought formed, she heard a car pull into the driveway. She glanced up briefly, then shrugged. Her father would take care of whoever it was. But a few minutes later she heard footsteps coming toward the back of the house and then someone opening the back gate.

She sat up and looked around. A tremor slithered down her spine as Kent stepped onto the deck.

He stopped. "Hi," he said.

"Hi." She stood, reaching for her beach towel. She was glad he wasn't close enough to see how her hand trembled as she clutched her book. She held her towel protectively in front of her, feeling her near-nakedness and wishing she didn't feel so exposed. She also wished she'd listened to her instincts and gone inside five minutes ago.

Yet even as the wish formulated, she couldn't suppress a tiny spurt of pleasure as she looked at him. She'd always enjoyed looking at Kent, always thought he was one of the nicest-looking men she'd ever known. He wasn't movie-star handsome, but his appeal was timeless and pure male. Today he wore khaki walking shorts with lots of pockets and a pale yellow knit shirt, both of which set off his tan and emphasized his solid, athletic body. Large wraparound sunglasses covered his eyes and hid his expression from her. In his left hand he carried a dark briefcase, which should have looked incongruous with his casual outfit but didn't.

"I rang the doorbell, but no one answered," he said. He gestured with the briefcase. "I brought some papers over for Lee and Mom to sign."

Allison, still feeling awkward, walked slowly toward him. "That's funny. Dad's inside. He was working in the study last time I saw him."

"Where's my mother?"

"She's out showing houses."

"Oh. I guess I should have called first. But you said Lee's here?"

"Yes. I—I'll go find him for you, if you like."

"No, that's okay. I've already bothered you. I can go find him myself." But he made no move to go.

"I'm going in, anyway. I think I've had enough sun for today," Allison said.

He removed his sunglasses, and his clear blue gaze slowly inspected her. "You always did sunburn easily," he said softly.

Heat suffused Allison as their gazes locked. Unspoken thoughts shimmered in the air between them. Remembrances of past intimacies, of shared experiences, of happy times together, flooded Allison's mind, and she knew Kent was remembering, too. Her heart picked up speed, and she wished she could give voice to her regrets. She wished she could say something, anything that would clear the air between them.

Just then the back door opened, and the moment was gone. Her father walked outside. "Kent!" he said. "Was that you ringing the doorbell?"

Kent smiled, the first time he'd smiled today, and pain welled into Allison's chest. She would give anything to have Kent smile at her that way again, with spontaneity and warmth and pleasure. "Yeah," he said. "Where were you?"

"Trapped on the phone. I'd just placed a call to Pieter Koenig in Amsterdam and was waiting for him to come on the line. Sorry about that."

"That's okay. I brought the revised papers we talked about."

"You didn't have to do that. I told you I'd come and pick them up at your office."

Kent shrugged. "I'm on my way to Dusty's, so it was no trouble at all."

Lee grinned. "You still hanging out at that saloon?"

Kent chuckled. "Yeah. Some things never change."

Today everything Kent said reminded Allison of the past. She remembered the one time he'd taken her to Dusty's, a favorite haunt of his law school days. She hadn't been crazy about the place, and she'd made no secret of her dislike. He hadn't taken her again. Oh, God, she'd been such a snob then. It was a wonder he had ever loved her at all. Suddenly she couldn't bear to stand out here in his company another moment. "I—I'll leave you two to discuss your business," she said, avoiding Kent's eyes. "I'm going in."

"I'm not staying, so don't let me run you off," Kent said, his tone stiff. He removed a manila folder from his briefcase and handed it to her father.

Her gaze darted to his. "You're not running me off." But the expression in his eyes told her he knew she was lying. And when her gaze drifted back to her father, she knew he knew it, too. "I told you. I've been in the sun too long."

Kent didn't answer, but she could feel his eyes on her as she walked to the back door. She opened it. "Be sure to sign these in the presence of two witnesses who are not related to you" were the last words she heard Kent say before she closed the door behind her.

"Kent, are you paying attention?"

Kent looked at Christina, who sat across from him in the law library. "Yeah, sure, did you say something?"

Christina rolled her eyes. "I not only said something, I said it *twice.*" She frowned. "You've been preoccupied all day. What's wrong with you?"

He shrugged. "Just tired, I guess."

Her frown deepened. "Tired? But you said you didn't do anything this weekend. You didn't even work."

Was it his imagination, or was her tone accusatory? "I've put in more than my share of hours since we started work on this case. I think I'm entitled to a weekend off."

"You don't have to get so defensive. I just made a comment, that's all."

"Sounded more like an accusation to me."

"What *did* you do while I was gone?"

Jesus, she was beginning to act as if she owned him. "I told you. Nothing much."

"But what, specifically?" She tapped her gold pen against the open reference book sitting in front of her. Her long, painted nails were the exact shade of red as her suit and her lipstick. Always perfectly turned out, Christina exuded confidence and power. For some reason, this fact irritated him today, when earlier this had been something that he'd admired. "Did you play tennis with Bobby? Did you go out Saturday night?"

He stared at her. Her gray eyes stared back. Women, he thought in disgust, he was beginning to feel they weren't worth the aggravation. What was her problem? She'd never quizzed him like this before. And he didn't care for it. Not one little bit. He forced himself to keep his voice mild. "I didn't know I had to give you a report. What do you want? A detailed summary? Shall I write everything down? Eight fifty-five, left for the tennis game. Nine-fifteen, started the game."

Her eyes narrowed. When she spoke, her voice was tight. "You don't have to be so sarcastic, Kent. I just asked a simple question."

"First I'm defensive, now I'm sarcastic. Make up your mind."

Her jaw hardened, her eyes glittering like smoky diamonds. Hard, smoky diamonds. "I don't care for your tone of voice."

He shrugged.

"You can be a real bastard when you try, you know that?"

He smiled. "All this name-calling isn't very professional, Christina. I just don't happen to like this interrogation." Still calm. Still cool.

"I'll ignore that crack about me not being professional," she snapped. "And if you don't want to tell me what you were doing, fine. Don't tell me."

"I thought we had an understanding. I don't run your life, and you don't run mine."

"Did you go over to your mother's this weekend?"

Oh, so that was it. "As a matter of fact, I did." He'd be damned if he'd explain further.

Her smile was wry. "I thought so."

"Look, I don't know what in hell you're thinking, but whatever it is, you're wrong. The only reason I resisted giving you a blow-by-blow account of my weekend was because I was trying to make a point." The point being, you do not own me. Yet.

"Oh, I got your point," she said, fury written all over her beautiful face. She laid down her pen. "Your point came through loud and clear. Now could we please get back to business? We have a lot more work to do before we can call it a day. Or would you prefer I finish up so you can go and do whatever it is you're doing that you don't want to discuss?"

Kent decided he would not rise to her bait again. "Good idea," he said. "Where were we?"

She looked as if she wanted to say something else. Instead, she shrugged and said, "We were deciding which of us should track down and interview the members of the design team for the Wild Rider and which of us should interview Petrowski's friends and family.''

''Why don't you take the family, and I'll take the design team?'' Kent suggested.

''Why?''

''You're better at interviewing family than I am.''

''I'm also better at ferreting out dirt.''

Kent winced. What she said was true. Christina had a nose for dirt. Whenever a potential witness had something to hide, she usually sensed it. So it wasn't surprising she was suspicious about his feelings for Allison.

Kent, on the other hand, wanted to believe everyone. You'd think, after his disastrous experience at the storefront, he would be more cynical and less apt to take people at face value. Well, hell, he *was* more cynical, but he still had a long way to go before he could match Christina. His tendency to want to believe the best of people was a bone of contention between them. More than once she had accused him of being squeamish. Of not having the guts to go for the jugular.

Sometimes Kent wondered if she was right. Take the Wilder case, for instance. No matter how many times he told himself all his loyalty should lie with Emmett Wilder, who was, after all, his firm's client and the one paying the bills, Kent found himself identifying with Shelley Petrowski. He had never even met the woman, had only seen pictures of her at her husband's funeral, but the pictures had haunted him. He couldn't understand how anyone seeing the young widow with her tear-streaked face, holding tightly on to the hand of her three-year-old daughter and cradling her infant son in her other arm, could be anything but sympathetic.

He sighed. It wasn't his job to worry about Shelley Petrowski. It was his job to find evidence to back up Emmett Wilder's claim that his company was not at fault in Greg Petrowski's unfortunate accident.

"Honestly, Kent, you're doing it again!" Christina said, exasperation dripping from her voice. "What is your problem today?"

"Sorry. I was thinking about the case."

"What about it?"

He shrugged. "Nothing. Just thinking about who I'll talk to first." There was no point in telling Christina his doubts. She wouldn't understand. In her mind, everything was black or white. Either something was important because it would help your client's case, or it was irrelevant because it wouldn't. Period. End of discussion. There was no room for gray areas in Christina's thinking. And she would be quick to tell him there was no room for gray areas in his thinking, either.

Later that afternoon, in his office, Kent rubbed his forehead wearily. He really should stay late tonight. He'd goofed off enough this weekend.

But once again he didn't feel like working. He wanted to go home, change into comfortable clothes, have a cold beer and plop down in front of the TV set. Mindless stuff. He began to cram papers into his briefcase. He would compromise. He'd leave now, but he'd try to get some work done at home tonight.

Just as he snapped his briefcase shut, his intercom buzzed. "Mr. Sorensen," his secretary said, "Mr. Gabriel is on line one."

"Thanks, Loretta." Kent punched the button for line one. "Lee?"

"Hello, Kent. Sorry to bother you at work."

"That's okay." He wondered what his stepfather wanted. He rarely called Kent at work. "Is everything okay with the wills?"

"Yes, yes, everything's fine with the wills. That's not why I called. I wanted to talk to you about something, and I happened to be thinking about it right now so decided to call you while it was on my mind."

"Sounds serious."

"Not serious, but it's important. At least to me." Lee hesitated for a moment, then said slowly, "It's about Allison."

"Oh?" Kent said cautiously. Allison was a subject he preferred not to talk about, especially with Lee. He had successfully avoided thinking about her today. And that's the way he wanted to keep it.

"Ordinarily I try to stay out of yours and Allison's personal lives. . . ."

Kent waited. He remembered when once that hadn't been true.

"But these are unusual circumstances," Lee continued. "Look, Kent, I'm not going to beat around the bush. I can see that you're constrained around Allison. It's been obvious to both me and your mother that you haven't forgiven or forgotten what happened between the two of you."

Kent stiffened. "Well, I'm sorry you feel that—"

"Now don't get defensive," Lee said. "I'm not blaming you for anything."

"Sure sounded that way to me." Kent knew he was reacting badly, but he couldn't seem to help himself. After all, he wasn't the one who had run out on Allison. He wasn't the one in the wrong here. *She* was the one who had caused all their problems, so he had a perfect right to be angry.

"Come on, Kent, be fair," his stepfather said mildly. "You know your mother and I love both you and Allison. But right now Allison needs our help and support more than you do. She's going through a difficult time and she doesn't need more stress in her life. She needs less."

"Meaning?"

"Meaning your attitude isn't helping things. If it's obvious to me and your mother that you're still holding a grudge against her, don't you think Allison realizes it, too? It was obvious to me yesterday, seeing the way she acted when you came to the house, that she *does* feel your animosity. Do you really want her to have more to worry about and feel guilty about than she already does? Can't you be a little understanding and put your personal differences aside?" Lee's voice took on a gentle, chiding tone. "Allison needs all her resources to deal with Marianne's problems. She needs her family behind her. Supporting her."

"Maybe it would be best, then, if I just stayed away from the house completely."

Lee didn't answer for a long moment. Then he said slowly, "Well, that wasn't exactly what I had in mind. Look, Allison really needs a friend right now. I was hoping that instead of staying away, you would make a real effort to be that friend."

Kent took a deep breath. "Sir, you know I respect you. You know I'd do just about anything for you. But you're asking too much this time. If you think I'm upsetting Allison, I'll stay away. But that's all I can do. Because there's no way she and I are ever going to be friends."

Chapter Four

Allison looked around Marcy Bartlett's kitchen. Marcy and Joel had completely redone the old West University house they'd bought two years ago. In keeping with the Colonial design, the kitchen was red, white and blue and had an old-fashioned country flavor.

Marcy had been Allison's best friend since they'd met at camp as ten-year-olds and recognized a kindred spirit. Allison had missed Marcy during the years she'd spent in Paris. They hadn't had much contact, mainly because Allison hadn't wanted Marcy to know how unhappy she was.

Today both women were seated at the large round maple table that dominated the room. They had large glasses of iced tea in front of them, and Marcy had set out some thin slices of lemon pound cake. As they talked, Marcy held Marianne.

"Hi, cutie," she said softly. "Are you gonna give me a smile?"

The baby cooed.

Allison felt like hugging Marcy. Some days Marianne's color was worse than others. Some people were scared off by it and were afraid to handle the baby. But Marcy was a natural and treated Marianne as if there weren't anything wrong with her. Nikki had been the same way, and Allison was grateful.

"I love your kitchen," Allison said.

"Thanks." Marcy grimaced, her nose wrinkling. "This kitchen's my consolation prize."

Allison frowned. "Consolation prize?"

"Uh-huh. Because I can't get pregnant, and Joel wanted to take my mind off that depressing fact."

"Oh, Marce, I didn't know...." Allison said softly, her heart going out to her friend, whose freckled face and normally bright eyes both held traces of pain. "But listen, it just takes some women longer than others—"

"I know. But we've been trying for three years."

"Oh." Here Allison had been envying Marcy because she had a devoted husband whom she adored, a home of her own and a settled life. All of which proved you could never really tell anything about anyone from the surface. Outwardly it might look as if a person had everything going for them. Inwardly they might be uncertain or unhappy or any one of a dozen negative emotions. "Have you thought about adoption?"

"Yes, Joel and I have talked about it, but, well, Joel's an only child, and his parents are kind of hung up on us having a baby of our own."

Allison nodded sympathetically.

Marcy shrugged, her light blue eyes thoughtful. "I haven't given up hope. And if I don't get pregnant, I'm going to push to adopt." She turned her gaze back to Marianne. "I want a baby so badly. You're so lucky to have Marianne." She nuzzled the baby's forehead. "She's so beautiful, even though she's sick." Then her face took on a stricken look. "Oh, Allison, I'm sorry! I completely forgot about Jean Luc."

"That's okay. Believe me, I am lucky to have Marianne, and I know it." She hesitated, then hurriedly, before she could change her mind, said, "I—I haven't told anyone else this, but Jean Luc and I didn't have the best of relationships."

"Oh?"

Allison sighed, looking away from her friend's penetrating gaze. "I guess I married him on the rebound. And you know what they say about marrying in haste...."

"You sounded as if you were in love with him when you called me to tell me you were getting married," Marcy said softly.

"I know now that I was simply dazzled by him. He was so good-looking, so dark and dangerous and sexy. And he paid attention to me. He made me feel really special. I needed that. My ego was bruised after what happened with Kent."

Marcy nodded. "I wondered when the conversation would get around to Kent."

Allison swallowed. She hadn't meant to mention Kent's name. Or had she?

"Have you seen him yet?"

Allison nodded. "Twice." She fiddled with her iced-tea glass, drawing circles in the condensation. "My dad and Diana had a barbecue on the fourth, and he came...with a gorgeous blonde on his arm. And then yesterday he stopped by the house, and I saw him for a minute."

"And?"

"And what?"

"How did you feel?"

Allison thought about lying. But that wasn't why she'd introduced the subject, and she knew it. She wanted to tell Marcy everything she couldn't tell her father. Or her stepmother. Or anyone else. She wanted her friend to give her advice. To tell her everything would be all right. And it seemed fitting to confide in Marcy, because she and Joel, who was Kent's best friend, had introduced the two of them. Ironically, Allison thought with a start, at a Fourth of July barbecue. Why had that fact just occurred to her?

"I—I felt awkward and nervous and miserable. My—my heart was beating like a tom-tom, my hands were sweaty, and my throat was dry. I felt like crying, and I didn't know what to say."

Marcy grinned. "Gee. Is that all? And here I thought you might have cared!"

Allison laughed, but she could feel tears forming at the back of her eyes, and she blinked several times to try to keep them at bay. But she couldn't, and suddenly, without warning, she began to cry. She bit her bottom lip, furious with herself, and scrabbled around in her pocket for a tissue. "Damn," she said. "What's wrong with me?"

"Oh, honey," Marcy said. "You're still in love with him, aren't you?"

"No!" Allison dabbed at her eyes, then blew her nose. "I'm not still in love with him. I—I just... Oh, shoot, I don't know! I feel so strange around him. It—it hurts to see him." She swallowed, concentrating on keeping the tears back. "Oh, this is so stupid. I don't know why I'm acting like such a fool."

Marcy laughed again, but her eyes were filled with sympathy. "Allison, can I ask you something?"

Allison blew her nose again. "Of course."

"Do—do you ever regret what you did?"

Allison sighed, looking down at her hands for a moment. "You mean running out on Kent?"

"Yes."

Allison's gaze met Marcy's once again. "Yes, I regret it. I regretted it from almost the first moment I did it."

"Then why? Why didn't you just turn around and come back? You know he wanted you to."

"Oh, God, Marce, I don't know! I was young and stupid and stubborn and pigheaded. Who knows why anyone does anything?" She twisted the tissue in her hands. "And I guess I felt that Kent didn't love me enough."

"Didn't love you enough! How can you say that? Kent was absolutely bonkers over you. Why, Joel and I have talked about it a million times, how Kent was so nuts about you he couldn't see straight."

Allison shrugged. "Obviously he didn't love me enough to take the job with Keating & Shaw."

"But, Allison, the same could be said for you. You didn't love him enough to marry him no matter what he decided to do."

Allison nodded. "I know. Don't you think I've told myself the same thing dozens of times? I was selfish and wrong." She sighed heavily. "Unfortunately I can't go back and change things."

"It's a dirty, rotten shame that things turned out the way they did. You two were so good together. I just couldn't understand why you couldn't work things out."

"I don't know. I guess I felt I came second, and maybe Kent felt that way, too."

"I don't think you came second with Kent. It's just that he was so idealistic. He'd dreamed of opening his storefront law office for years, and he couldn't relinquish that dream."

"Yet barely four years later, he's done just that," Allison said. Suddenly the unhappiness and confusion and, yes, betrayal, she'd been feeling ever since learning of Kent's abandonment of his storefront practice nearly overwhelmed her. "Why did he do it, Marcy? Why was he unable to do for me what he did later, anyway? All these years I've been feeling so guilty...so sorry about hurting him, but at least I could take comfort from the fact that his life was on the right track...that he was doing what he was always meant to do. And then I come home and discover he's gone to work for Keating & Shaw after all!" She fell silent, overwhelmed by the futility of it all. Why had they both had to suffer? Had everything been in vain?

Marcy, eyes compassionate, said slowly, "I don't know, Allison. Things change. Maybe your leaving Kent made him see things differently."

Allison rubbed her head. "It doesn't matter now. It's no use second-guessing. It's all over with. Nothing can change the past. Now I've got to stop thinking about Kent and what happened between us and concentrate on Marianne."

Marcy looked down at the baby, whose eyes were drifting open and shut. "She's sleepy," she whispered.

"I know. I think I'd better be going."

"Oh, don't go yet!"

"I'd better." Allison stood. "And Marce?"

Marcy looked up.

"Please don't mention any of what I said about Kent to Joel."

Marcy frowned. "I wouldn't do that—"

"Yes, you would." Allison knew that Marcy and Joel told each other everything. "But promise me that this time you won't."

Marcy seemed about to say something else. Instead, she sighed. "Okay. I won't."

"Promise."

"Cross my heart."

Allison chuckled over their childhood pledge and reached for the baby.

Kent spent the day tracking the whereabouts of the six-member design team for the Wild Rider. Four of the designers were still employed by Wilder's. He made a check mark by their names. He would set up interviews with them for later in the week. He knew the plaintiff's attorney would subpoena all of them for depositions, so he felt it was important to woodshed them first—slang for coaching them privately, as in taking them behind the woodshed and telling them what to say.

One of the designers had died of a heart attack two months earlier. Kent crossed his name off the list.

That left one—the senior member of the team—Armand Brasselli. In checking Brasselli's personnel file, Kent saw the man had retired in January and moved to Poway, California. There was even an address in the files because Brasselli was collecting early retirement. Kent made a note to ask his secretary to try to set up a time when Kent could fly out there to interview him.

After that he made a list of all the possible questions the designers would be asked by the opposition. Once he had talked with the designers, he would help them formulate answers, as well as tell them what not to say. Since the plaintiff's case was based on the theory that Wilder had known there was a design problem, Kent figured the design team would play a big part in the trial.

By the end of the day, Kent left the office with a satisfied feeling, knowing he'd accomplished a lot.

Tuesday night he met Joel Bartlett, who worked for the rival firm of MacAllister, Amann and Royer, for drinks at their favorite downtown pub. As usual Joel was sitting at the bar, and Kent slid onto a bar stool next to him.

"So how was your day?" Joel asked.

"Busy. What about you?"

Joel shrugged. "Boring." He drank some of his beer. "I'm thinking about looking for another job."

Kent frowned. "Why? There's only one other firm in town that compares to yours, and that's mine. Why change?"

Joel sighed. "I don't think I'm cut out to work for a big law firm. I want to do a lot of different kinds of things, and you know how it is with the big guns. New guys like us just do grunt work. Same old, same old. All day, every day."

Kent nodded sympathetically. Boredom was a common complaint among his contemporaries from law school. It took a lot of years of grunt work and proving yourself before you were allowed to handle anything even remotely challenging. He knew he was lucky to be on the Wilder case. At least the case itself was interesting, even if he probably would not be assigned anything other than research and interviewing.

"Why don't we start our own firm?" Joel offered.

"No way," Kent said. "I was an entrepreneur once, remember?"

"That was different. Think about it, Kent. You, me, Michael. The three of us together—why, we'd be unbeatable!" Joel's eyes shone with enthusiasm.

Kent just shook his head. He was sitting in the catbird seat at Keating & Shaw. He would soon be in the six-figure income bracket. Starting a firm of their own would mean struggling for years. Although . . . he had to admit the thought of working with Joel and Michael Berry, another young lawyer they'd hung around with all through law school, held a lot of appeal. At one time he'd have jumped at the chance to do something like this. But now, well, he'd learned his lesson. "No, I don't think so. We'd be giving up a sure thing for a shot in the dark," he said. "I don't want to risk it."

"Yeah, you're probably right," Joel said morosely. "Marcy'd probably kill me if I mentioned it. Now that we've bought that house, we need every penny I earn."

Kent nodded.

They fell silent for a few minutes, then Joel said, "So Allison's back, I hear."

"Yeah." Kent did not want to discuss Allison. Maybe if he didn't elaborate, Joel would drop the subject.

"Have you seen her?"

Kent sighed. Joel wasn't going to drop the subject. "Yeah, I've seen her," he said reluctantly.

Joel started to say something else when the bartender walked up to them. "What'll you guys have?" he asked, wiping the bar in front of them.

"I'll have a light beer," Joel said.

"Me, too," Kent said.

"So how'd she look?" Joel asked when the bartender had served them and walked away.

Kent shrugged. "Older. Thinner." He kept his voice as noncommittal and impersonal as he could. He wanted nothing so much as to talk about something else. Anything else.

"Yeah, well, that's understandable. She's had a rough time. Even so, I'll bet she's still gorgeous."

Kent shrugged again. "I guess so."

"You guess so! You suddenly grow a pair of blinders?" Joel chuckled at his sally. Then his smile grew sly. "I can't believe you're that indifferent. You never were before."

"Yeah, well, times change."

"Not that much."

"*I've* changed."

Joel took a swallow of beer, then he grinned. "Like I said, not that much." He nudged Kent. "Come on. Tell me the truth. You're not as immune as you pretend to be."

Kent ignored him and drank some beer himself.

"She came over to visit with Marcy yesterday...." Joel said slowly. He drank more beer and grabbed a handful of peanuts from the dish in front of them.

Kent refused to rise to the bait. He said nothing.

"Marcy said she's different."

Why couldn't Joel talk about something else? "Yeah, well, we've all changed. Say, did you see the Astros' game last night?"

"Nope." Joel ate a few peanuts. "Marcy said Allison's really grown up. Matured."

Kent sighed heavily. He turned to Joel, fixing him with a steady look. His friend looked back. "Joel, I know what you're trying to do, and it's not going to work. I don't want to discuss Allison. Now, can we talk about something else?''

"Oh, jeez, sorry, buddy. I wasn't thinking, I guess. If the subject makes you uncomfortable, sure, we can talk about something else."

If Kent hadn't known Joel so well, he might have believed that bland innocence in his expression and his tone of voice. "The subject doesn't make me uncomfortable. I just happen not to be interested."

"Hey, no problem. Don't get riled up."

"I'm *not* riled up!" Kent said with more force than he'd intended. "Why does everyone persist in trying to shove the topic of Allison down my throat?" Kent took a swig of beer. "Damn it!" he said as he set the bottle down. "I couldn't care less what she says or does."

Joel raised his eyebrows.

The lively strains of a Clint Black song filled the silence between them. Why Clint Black? Kent wondered. Was everyone and everything conspiring to remind him of Allison and their past relationship? Clint Black had always been one of her favorite performers, and Kent had taken her to see him in person once. It had been a wonderful evening, and at the end of it, when they'd kissed good night, she had said, "I love you so much, Kent. You're so good to me."

Kent sighed again. Joel was right. He was bothered by Allison, and he didn't like it when anyone discussed her. "Listen, Joel, I'm sorry," he said. "I guess I'm touchy where she's concerned."

"It's okay. I understand."

"No, I'm not sure you do." Hell, how could Joel understand when Kent didn't understand himself?

"Listen. If you don't want to talk about her, it's okay. But, you know, you're going to be thrown into her company whether you want to be or not."

"I know, and I've got to learn to handle it better." He tapped his fingertips on the bar. "Lee called me yesterday. He asked me to try to mend fences with her. He said she's really going through a bad time right now."

"Yeah. Marcy told me."

"So what else did Marcy tell you?" In spite of his protestations to the contrary, Kent wondered if Marcy and Allison had discussed him.

"Nothing much."

"Oh, come on. Marcy tells you everything."

Joel's eyes were impossible to read in the darkness of the bar. "Well, not this time. In fact, she was suspiciously closemouthed." He grinned. "So suspiciously, I finally asked her about it. You know what she said?"

"No, what?"

"She said Allison had made her promise not to tell me about their conversation."

Later, as Kent lay in bed and tried to fall asleep, he kept thinking about Joel's statement and wondering what it was the two women had discussed that Allison didn't want Joel to know.

"I called Kent yesterday," Lee said as Diana slipped into bed beside him.

"Oh? What about?"

"I wanted to talk to him about Allison."

Lee could feel her stiffen beside him. "What about Allison?" she asked quietly.

"I just told him Allison could really use a friend about now."

There was silence for a moment, and Lee could almost hear the wheels turning in Diana's mind. "I'm not sure it's realistic to think Kent and Allison could ever be friends, Lee," she said slowly.

"If Kent makes an effort, they can be."

She turned on her side to face him and gently touched his forearm. As it had never failed to do in the three and a half years they'd been married, her touch sent a tingle of pleasure through him. "Honey, do you think it's fair to put that kind of pressure on Kent?" She paused. "I know why you did it. You think Allison's under too much stress, and you want to make things easier for her. Well, I do, too, but none of her problems are Kent's fault, you know."

He laid his hand over hers. "I know that. But if they're ever going to be comfortable around each other, Kent will have to make the first move."

"Well...what did Kent say when you talked to him?"

"At first he tried to deny that there was a problem between them."

"And then ..." Diana prompted.

"He said pretty much what you said. That he and Allison could never be friends."

He could feel her shrug.

"I was hoping maybe you'd talk to him," Lee suggested.

"Me! Absolutely not. This is none of our business, Lee. I understand why you felt you had to try. After all, Allison's your daughter, and it's natural for you to be concerned about her, but don't expect me to get involved."

"I thought you cared about Allison."

She stiffened. "I do care about Allison. But I also care about Kent. She hurt him once, Lee. And once is more than enough."

Allison couldn't sleep Tuesday night. All she could think about was that at eight o'clock the next morning, Marianne would be prepped and already half-asleep in preparation for the heart catheterization.

Diana and Lee had both arranged to be off all day and were planning to accompany Allison and Marianne to the hospital. Allison would always be grateful for their support. Right now she wasn't sure how she would have survived if she hadn't had them to count on.

All day she'd tried not to think about the test. All day she'd tried not to think about what she would do if Marianne's prognosis wasn't good. All day she'd tried not to think about how she would survive if Marianne didn't make it.

Allison didn't want to think these gloomy thoughts. She had always believed in the power of positive thinking. But she was also a realist. She always had been. In fact, her pragmatic approach to life was what had caused her problems with Kent.

Kent was a romantic. Allison wasn't. All her romanticism had evaporated when her mother had died when Allison was just a teenager. Allison had adored her effervescent, beautiful mother, and when her mother had told her that she'd been diagnosed with breast cancer, she'd downplayed the significance of the diagnosis. She'd told Allison that the malignancy would be removed and all would be well.

All hadn't been well.

The malignancies couldn't all be removed. The spread of the cancer had been too fast and too pervasive.

Marianne Gabriel had only lived two months after her surgery.

And Allison had never been the same. As she stood beside her father while her mother's coffin had been lowered into the ground, she'd realized that all the positive thinking and romantic notions in the world wouldn't do a bit of good when faced with the harsh realities of life.

But no matter how many times Allison told herself this, she simply couldn't imagine life without her baby daughter. She refused to think about how she'd cope if the worst happened.

The worst won't happen, she told herself fiercely. *I won't let it happen.*

At six-thirty Wednesday morning, Allison and Marianne were safely ensconced in the back seat of Diana's Mercedes. The trip to the medical center only took twenty minutes. By seven o'clock Allison was signing the admission papers, and Marianne was whisked off to begin preparation for her test.

At nine o'clock Marianne was wheeled into surgery, and Allison, Lee and Diana were seated in the waiting room.

At ten o'clock, after several cups of coffee, Allison gave up all pretense of reading the magazine in her hands and anxiously watched the clock.

At ten-thirty Dr. Richardson, the heart surgeon, finally entered the waiting area. "Mrs. Fornier?"

"Yes." Allison stood, clasping her purse tightly. Her mouth had gone dry. The doctor looked so solemn. Her heart suddenly stopped beating. Within seconds her father and Diana had joined her, one on either side. Dr. Richardson nodded to them, then turned his dark gaze back to Allison.

"Is Marianne all right?" Allison asked. *Please, God. Please let her be all right.*

"Yes. She's fine right now. However, the test showed that the blockage of the pulmonary artery is as I anticipated. Your daughter will definitely need open-heart surgery to correct this problem."

Even though Allison thought she'd been prepared for this edict, her heart began to pound and her knees suddenly felt weak. "Wh-when?" she managed to ask.

Allison's father laid a comforting hand on her shoulder, and Diana slipped her arm around Allison's waist.

"Well," Dr. Richardson continued, "right now we'll wait and watch. The older she is, the better her prognosis. But she'll require careful monitoring. The most crucial problem would be congestive heart failure. If her color should worsen or she should have trouble breathing, you should, of course, call us immediately."

Allison listened as the doctor went on to explain that Allison would have to keep the baby as quiet as possible because every time Marianne got too excited or upset, her oxygen level would go down, compounding her problems. The French doctors had said much the same thing, but then she hadn't wanted to listen. Now she had no choice.

"H-how long will Marianne have to stay in the hospital now, Doctor?" she asked.

"There are a couple more tests we want to do tomorrow morning. But you can take her home after that."

He went on to say that Marianne would be in recovery for about an hour, then, if all was okay, she would be brought back to her room in the Pediatric ICU.

The rest of the day passed in a blur. Allison did what she was told to do, but all she could think about was the upcoming heart surgery and the severity of Marianne's problems. She felt as if a tremendous weight were pressing down on her chest as a great fear overwhelmed her. All afternoon she sat in the waiting area, and when she was allowed into Marianne's room for ten minutes each hour, she stood by Marianne's crib and watched her sleeping daughter. When her father or her stepmother talked to her, she answered, but her answers were automatic. Her entire attention was focused on the baby.

Marianne stirred off and on during the afternoon but didn't wake entirely until about four o'clock. Allison wished desperately she could hold the baby, but as long as Marianne was attached to so many tubes and wires, that was impossible. In addition to the cardiac monitor and intravenous, the baby was being given oxygen by nasal cannula—two little prongs attached to her nose. It hurt Allison to look at her, and countless times during the day she wished she could switch places with the baby. She would gladly have endured all the pain to save Marianne from suffering any more than she had already.

About five-thirty Lee and Diana headed for the cafeteria again, but Allison didn't want to go. She knew she'd never get food down. With a weary sigh she walked to the window of the waiting area, which overlooked a courtyard. Down below she could see several people sitting on a stone bench under a small redbud tree. Dotted in clusters around the courtyard were bunches of white-and-purple periwinkles. The July sun beat down, firing the courtyard with bright light.

Everything looked so normal outside. No one out there gave any indication that they might be thinking of the life-and-death struggles going on inside these stone walls. Lost in her thoughts, Allison gazed out the window.

"Allison . . ."

She whirled around to stare at Kent, who stood in the doorway. For a moment she was speechless. "Wh-what are you doing here?" she blurted. Immediately she wanted to kick herself. "I—I'm sorry. I didn't mean that the way it sounded. I was just so surprised to see you. How'd you get in?" Even the waiting area outside the Intensive Care Unit was limited to family members.

He smiled ruefully, advancing into the room. He was dressed in a charcoal pin-striped suit, white shirt and dark red tie. She realized he'd probably come from work. "I told them I was your brother," he said. He shrugged. "It wasn't really a lie."

Allison nodded, still stunned by his appearance.

"How's Marianne doing?" He inclined his head toward the double doors leading into the ICU.

"So far, she's doing okay." They were both still standing, facing one another. "Listen, why don't we sit down?" she suggested.

Once they were seated, Kent said, "Where're Lee and my mother?"

"Eating dinner in the cafeteria."

"Oh." He studied her, his blue eyes solemn. "How are you doing?"

Allison shrugged. "I'm okay." She went on to explain what Dr. Richardson had told them.

"That's tough," Kent said softly, and the sympathy in his voice touched her.

"How'd you know where we were?" Allison finally asked.

"I called my mother's office, and Carla told me." Carla was Diana's receptionist.

"It—it was good of you to come." She lifted her gaze until it met his.

His eyes held an expression she didn't understand. She could feel her heart beating too fast.

"Kent, I—"

"Allison—"

They both spoke at once.

"Yes?" she said.

"No, you go first," he said.

There were so many things she wanted to say. So many things she didn't dare say. "I—I'm sorry for everything," she said, blurting it out before she lost her nerve. "I'm sorry I hurt you."

He stared at her. His eyes were so blue. They reminded her of an October sky, clear and bright and intense. She wished he'd say something.

"Do—do you think you can ever forgive me? Is it possible for us to be friends?" She was determined to settle this here and now. If he could never forgive her, it was better to know it.

"I don't know," he finally said. "But I'm—I'm willing to try if you are."

Something warm and sweet rushed through her at his words. "Oh, Kent," she said, "except for Marianne getting well, there's nothing I want more in this world."

Chapter Five

For the next couple of days, Kent couldn't get his conversation with Allison out of his mind. He kept remembering the way she'd looked when he'd seen her in the hospital. The dark shadows that looked like smudges under her eyes. How haunted her expression was. How much he had wanted to take her into his arms and comfort her.

He told himself his reaction was perfectly normal. That anyone, seeing how worried Allison was, seeing how tiny and helpless Marianne looked, would have felt the same way. He also told himself the only reason he'd gone to the hospital at all was that he hadn't wanted to disappoint Lee. Ever since their conversation, when Kent had said he could never be Allison's friend, he'd felt like a jerk.

He knew she was at fault in their breakup. He knew he was perfectly justified in his answer to Lee's request. He even knew Lee was being a bit unreasonable in making the request.

Still, Kent had felt like a jerk.

So he'd gone to the hospital. And ever since, he hadn't been able to get the twin pictures of Allison and Marianne out of his mind.

He knew Marianne had gone home Thursday. He had casually called his mother on Friday and worked the conversation around to the baby. Diana had said yes, the baby was home and seemed to be doing fine. She'd explained what the doctor had told Allison about keeping her quiet.

"I was thinking of stopping by to see her," he said.

"That would be nice of you," his mother said.

He tried to gauge her reaction. Was she in favor of his visiting or not? He couldn't tell.

"Can you think of anything I could buy for the baby?" he continued. "I thought I'd bring her something."

His mother thought for a minute. "A cuddly stuffed animal?" she suggested.

On Saturday Kent decided to go into work early. He planned to work until about two o'clock, then go shopping for something for the baby. He would take the gift over to his mother's house on his way home.

When he arrived at work at eight o'clock Saturday morning, Christina was already there. She grinned at him, a gleam of triumph shining in her eyes.

He pushed aside his irritation. He and Christina had been playing this unacknowledged game for weeks—each one trying to beat the other one into the office. It seemed to Kent that no matter how early he got there, Christina was always there first. Kent had finally decided that being the victor in this subtle game of one-upmanship wasn't worth the aggravation, so now he came to work when he was ready to come, no matter when he thought Christina might be there. If she wanted to spend her time trying to best him, fine. Obviously she felt she had something to prove. He didn't.

"Sleep in?" she asked lazily. She was leaning back in her chair, her long legs propped up on the conference table. Today she wore tight jeans and a striped knit top that hugged her body. Weekends were always casual at the office. Kent was wearing jeans, too, along with a dark cotton shirt and deck shoes.

"No," he said.

"I tried to call you last night." Swinging her legs down, she leaned forward and propped her elbows on the table. Papers were spread out in front of her.

"I know. I got your message." Kent tossed his brief-case on the table.

"Why didn't you call me back?" The question was voiced casually, but Kent knew it wasn't a casual question.

"I got home late." He knew she was dying to ask where he'd been. He refused to volunteer the information. It was none of her business. They were not engaged or anything close to it. "I'm going to go get a cup of coffee. Do you want some?" he said.

"No." She looked about to say something more, but she didn't.

Acting as if everything were perfectly normal, he walked out the door and down the hall to the coffee room. He'd be damned if he was going to let Christina make him feel guilty. He had nothing to feel guilty about. He poured himself a cup of coffee, added two sugars and stirred. He leaned back against the countertop and took a sip. He'd give her a few minutes before going back to the conference room.

"Hey, Kent, how's it going?"

Kent looked up, smiling at Paul Castleman, another of the younger associates at the firm. "Hey, Paul! It's going great. How's it going with you?"

Paul shrugged. "Okay, I guess. But I'm bored. I wish I'd get assigned to something exciting like the Wilder case. They've still got me doing deposition summaries on the capitol land-lease deal. You're a lucky son of a gun, you know that?"

Kent grinned. "You sound like Joel Bartlett. He said the same thing last night."

"So," Paul asked, "do you think you'll get to do any courtroom work?"

"Are you serious?" Associates never got to do courtroom work, and Paul knew it. The best Kent and Christina and Paul and others like them could hope for was an interesting case, because they would always be assigned to do legwork, which meant research and interviewing. Courtroom work was always done by the senior guns in the office. Kent was always amused when he watched TV shows where young lawyers in a firm actually got to try cases in court because he knew that kind of thing never happened in real life. It was simply there for dramatic effect. In truth, a young lawyer's life was usually very humdrum and monotonous.

Although—and he had no intention of telling Paul this —Colin Jamieson *had* dangled a carrot in front of Kent's nose more than once since he'd been assigned to work under him, saying things like "maybe we'll let you get your feet wet on this case because we've got plans for you, and this will be good experience." But Kent knew better than to disclose that kind of information.

Envy, jostling for position and back-stabbing were not unknown among the associates. There was no sense in shooting himself in the foot before he ever got out of the gate.

He and Paul talked for a few more minutes, then Kent headed back to the conference room. Christina looked up as he reentered. "I thought you got lost or something."

"Nope. Just ran into Paul Castleman."

For the next couple of hours, they worked quietly. About eleven o'clock Christina closed the reference book she'd been perusing and stretched. "I'm hungry," she announced.

Kent looked up. "Me, too. My stomach's been growling for at least an hour."

Christina grinned. "I know. I heard it. Want to send out for pizza, or should we go out for lunch?"

"We'd better send out because I've got to leave about two o'clock." Although he told himself he didn't have to explain, he added, "I've got some things to do this afternoon."

To his intense relief, she didn't question him. He watched as Christina stood and walked to the far end of the room, where she picked up the receiver of the phone sitting on the mahogany sideboard.

After a minute she asked, "What kind should I get? Pepperoni and mushroom?"

"Yeah, that sounds good."

Once the pizza was ordered, she rejoined him at the table. "They'll be here in about twenty minutes."

"Good." He reached for the reference book he'd been studying.

"Have you got plans for tonight?" she asked.

"Uh, no."

"Do you want to come to my place for dinner? I'll fix steak and onion rings," she said, naming one of his favorite meals.

"I . . . uh . . . sure."

She smiled happily. When two o'clock came, she bid him a cheerful goodbye. "I'll see you at seven," she said, blowing him a kiss as he gathered up his things.

As Kent walked out the door, he wondered why he felt so little enthusiasm for the coming evening.

Allison tucked Marianne into her crib in the pretty blue bedroom Diana had designated as the nursery and thought how glad she was they hadn't kept Marianne more than one night at the hospital. She'd hated the hospital atmosphere and was very glad to be home.

It was funny. She'd only been staying at her father's house for ten days, but she already thought of it as home. More so than she'd ever thought of her Paris apartment with Jean Luc.

Determinedly she pushed the thought of Jean Luc from her mind. Every time she thought about her late husband, she started to feel guilty again. And she didn't want to feel guilty. She'd finally started to feel better about herself now that she had apologized to Kent. She hoped he'd meant what he'd said about trying to rebuild a friendly relationship. She had half hoped he would stop by Thursday night when they got home from the hospital, but he hadn't. Maybe he would come by this weekend. She hoped so.

She smiled, thinking of Kent. He'd been so nice to her at the hospital. She wondered about his change in attitude. It had come so abruptly. One day he was cold and aloof around her. The next he had come to see Marianne and stayed talking to Allison for more than an hour.

What had happened to make him change? Allison suspected her father might have had something to do with Kent's attitude. She knew it would be entirely in character for her father to have talked to Kent about her. But that was all right. Anything that would help eliminate the awkwardness between them was welcome.

She was still thinking about Kent as she walked slowly downstairs, out to the big, high-ceilinged kitchen with its open beams and gleaming copper pots and dozens of plants.

Her father was the cook in the household, and he took great pride in his kitchen. Although he held a job of heavy responsibility as executive vice president of sales for Berringer, International, he had been known to cut a late meeting short because he was planning to make something complicated for dinner and wanted to get home and get started. Diana always laughed when she told people about Lee and his prowess in the kitchen. "That's why I married him," she would say, giving him a loving glance. "Because he kept me so well fed and I didn't want to go back to frozen dinners."

As Allison entered the kitchen, her father looked up. He was slicing onions at the counter. "Baby still sleeping?"

Allison nodded. "I thought maybe she'd wake up by now, but she's still conked out."

"Well, she's been through a lot in the past couple of days." Lee dumped the onions into a pot, added a little water and set the pot on the stove. He turned on the burner, then walked back to the counter, where he proceeded to peel and slice another large onion.

"What're you making?" Allison said. She sank into a chair at the table.

"French onion soup." He grinned at her. "I thought we'd have open-face cheese sandwiches, salad and the soup."

"Sounds wonderful." But Allison had had no real appetite for food in months.

"I'm trying to fatten you up," her father said.

"I know." He was concerned about her weight loss, and Allison wished she could reassure him. *My appetite will come back the minute I know the baby's out of danger.*

Just then the doorbell rang.

"Honey, would you get that?" Lee requested.

Allison nodded and got up, walking toward the front door. As she entered the spacious foyer, she could see a man's outline through the smoky glass panels on either side of the massive double walnut doors. As she got closer, she was sure the man was Kent. Her heart accelerated as she opened the door and he smiled down at her.

"Hi. The gate was locked so I had to come to the front door like real company," he said. He held a large wrapped package in his hands.

She returned his smile. "Come on in." Suddenly she was glad she'd worn her apricot sundress today. She knew the color looked good on her. "Dad's back in the kitchen."

"Where's Mom?"

"She went shopping with your grandmother."

Kent rolled his eyes. "I'll bet she was thrilled about that. You know what a pain Gran can be."

Allison chuckled. She and Kent had been engaged long enough for her to understand that Diana and her mother had a real love-hate relationship. Barbara Kent was a garrulous, cranky woman who was never satisfied with anything her children did or did not do for her. Once Diana had said in Allison's hearing that if her mother said "jump" and her daughters did, she'd then complain that they'd deserted her.

Kent followed her back to the kitchen. "Hey, Lee," he said. "You on kitchen detail again?"

"Always," Lee said. He was adding cans of beef broth to his soup pot. "Your mother really cracks the whip if I shirk my duty."

Allison smiled at the idea of anyone cracking the whip with her forceful father. Still, if anyone could do it, it would be Diana.

"Would you like something to drink?" she asked Kent.

"Have you got any iced tea?"

While she poured him a glass of tea, he sat at the kitchen table, stretching his long legs out in front of him. He set the package on the table.

Allison gave him a covert glance, admiring the way his dark cotton shirt fit his broad chest and the way the fabric of his jeans molded to his thighs.

"So Mom took Gran out, huh?" he said.

Lee grimaced. "Under duress, I might add."

Kent turned to Allison, who had reseated herself at the table. "Speaking of grandparents, how're yours doing?"

"They're fine. They're on safari in Africa right now."

"I would've thought nothing would keep them away now that you're back home."

Allison knew Kent was referring to the fact that her maternal grandparents, Howard and Jinx Marlowe, doted on her. She was their only grandchild, and from the time she was born, they had thought the sun rose and set on her. "They'd already left on this trip by the time I decided to come home."

"When are they due back?" Kent asked.

"They'll be back next Sunday, and I can't wait to see them." Her grandparents really were pretty special, she thought.

"What about your Aunt Elizabeth? She still living here in Houston?"

"Sort of. Right now she's in New Zealand."

"New Zealand! What's she doing there?"

Allison grinned. "She's got a new boyfriend. He owns a chain of newspapers in New Zealand, and she's his houseguest." Her Aunt Elizabeth was her mother's only sister and Allison's only aunt. At one time Allison had hoped her father and her aunt would get together, but that hope was dashed when Lee fell in love with Diana. Now, though, Allison was glad things had worked out the way they had. She finally realized that no one was ever going to replace her mother, and it had been foolish of her to think anyone could.

"Did you work today, Kent?" Lee asked. He carefully measured Worcestershire sauce into his soup, then added black pepper and salt.

"Yes, until about two. Then I had some errands to run and thought I'd stop by here before going home. See how Marianne is doing." He turned to Allison again. "Where is she?" He reached for the package. "I brought her something."

"Oh, thank you," Allison said, pleased by his thoughtfulness. "She's sleeping. She seems to be doing a lot of sleeping since she got home."

Disappointment clouded his eyes.

A rush of happiness flooded Allison at the realization that Kent cared about Marianne, that she was beginning to be important to him. "Do you want to go upstairs and see her?" she asked.

His eyes brightened. "I'd love to."

"Can I open the present first?"

"Sure."

Allison carefully unwrapped the box, discarding the pale yellow paper and ribbon. She parted the tissue paper inside. A gasp of pleasure escaped as she lifted out a beautiful mobile of baby animals in pastel colors. Smiling, she wound the mobile. The pure, sweet notes of "Someone to Watch over Me" floated in the air.

Her gaze met Kent's, and she smiled. "It's beautiful. Marianne will love it."

Five minutes later they stood side by side, looking down into Marianne's crib. Allison was acutely conscious of the warmth of Kent's arm brushing hers and the intimacy of being here, in the darkened nursery, with him.

Marianne slept on her side, her tiny fists clasped together under her chin. Her breathing was feather light, and her eyelashes rested like layered silk against her cheeks. Allison wondered what Kent was thinking. She wondered if he ever thought about the fact that Marianne could have been their baby, if Allison hadn't broken their engagement. Allison thought it. All the time.

Very gently Kent reached inside and touched her hand with his forefinger. Marianne stirred.

"Oops, sorry," he whispered. "I wasn't trying to wake her up."

"I know," Allison whispered back. "It's okay." They stood looking at the baby for a few more minutes, then, in silent agreement, turned and walked quietly out of the room.

Once they were safely outside, Kent said, "She's a wonderful baby."

"Thanks. I think so, too."

"You're lucky to have her."

Allison looked up at the wistful note in his voice. Their gazes met, and there was something about the expression in his eyes that caused Allison's heart to start beating like a piston again. For a long moment they said nothing, then the moment passed and they continued on their way downstairs.

Kent stayed for almost an hour. For most of that time, they sat in the kitchen and watched Lee finish up his dinner preparations. Then Kent glanced at the kitchen clock. "I'd better get going," he said, standing. "It's after five."

"Why don't you stay for dinner?" Lee suggested. "There's plenty."

Kent's glance slid to Allison. "I—I can't," he said with what sounded like real regret to her. "I've got plans."

He has a date, Allison thought, knowing she was right. He was probably taking that Christina somewhere. She fought to keep her expression neutral and said brightly, "Well, thanks for stopping by. And thank you again for the mobile."

Within minutes he was gone. But Allison couldn't banish him from her thoughts. All night long she kept wondering what he and Christina were doing at that exact moment. Then she'd get mad at herself. Did she really want to know?

Later that night, after Marianne was in bed for the night and Allison was lying in her own bedroom down the hall, she wondered if Kent and Christina would spend the night together.

The thought that they might gave her the emptiest feeling—a feeling she knew she had no right to have. She had no claims on Kent. She had broken their engagement a long time ago, and he did not belong to her. He would never belong to her. So she might as well get used to the idea that he would make love to other women.

She wished with all her heart she had allowed him to make love to her when they were engaged. At least now she'd have those memories.

She finally fell asleep. But her dreams were filled with images of Kent. She pictured them as they had been on the night of their engagement party. After the party was over, they'd walked in the backyard of her grandparents' estate. The two of them had ended up in the gazebo at the back of the property. It had been beautiful out, clear and warm, with millions of stars twinkling in the navy night. They had kissed and touched, and their kisses had become more heated, their breathing more rapid. Allison had finally pulled away, and soon after Kent had gone home.

But this time, as she relived the night in her dream, when Kent wanted to make love to her, she didn't push him away. They made love right there, on the floor of the gazebo, with the moonlight shining through the latticework and dappling their bodies, which soon became slick and hot and quivering with desire.

This time, when Kent touched her, she touched him back. When his fingers found the sensitive peaks of her breasts, she arched into his touch and begged him for more. When he found her most intimate places, she didn't push him away.

And when their passion reached its zenith, Allison moaned and cried Kent's name, waking herself up.

For a long time afterward, she couldn't fall back asleep.

Chapter Six

Kent wearily sank onto the bar stool. Joel wasn't there yet, but Kent knew he'd be along in a few minutes. Their Friday-night beer together was a standing ritual, much as Kent's Sunday-morning tennis game with Bobby Halloran had become.

Sure enough, less than five minutes later Joel plopped down on the seat beside him. "Man, it's hot out there!" he said. He mopped his forehead with his handkerchief. "I sure will be glad when summer's over."

"You say that every summer," Kent said.

The bartender walked up, and Joel placed his order, then turned to Kent. "You look tired. Rough week at work?"

"Not as far as work goes."

"So what's the problem?"

Kent hesitated, but only for a moment. He grimaced. "Christina."

Joel raised his eyebrows. "I thought things were really cooking between you two."

Kent sighed. "They were, but now they're getting . . . complicated. I . . . uh . . . I haven't spent much time with her the past couple of weeks, and she's sore."

"She'll get over it."

"Unfortunately until she does, it's affecting our working relationship."

Joel took a swallow of his beer. "Didn't I tell you it was a mistake to get involved with someone you work with?"

"Yeah, and I wish I'd listened."

"You know, there was a time when you were really hot to trot as far as Christina was concerned. Nothing was more important than seeing her."

"Things change."

Joel gave him a thoughtful look.

"I know what you're thinking," Kent said, "and you're wrong."

"How do you know what I'm thinking?"

"Allison has nothing to do with this," Kent said. But he couldn't quite meet Joel's eyes, and he wondered what his friend was thinking. "My attraction to Christina has just run its course."

Joel raised his eyebrows. "Okay."

Kent gave him a defiant look. "Well, that does happen, you know!"

"I didn't say it didn't."

Kent stared into his beer bottle. "I thought you were my friend," he said morosely.

Joel chuckled. "I am your friend."

"Then why're you giving me such a hard time?"

"I'm not giving you a hard time. I'm just trying to get you to face the truth. That's what friends are supposed to do."

"No, they're not. They're supposed to be sympathetic. Say things like 'Yeah, you're right.'"

"Yeah, you're right," Joel said obediently, but there was laughter in his voice.

Kent continued to stare glumly at his beer. He wished he could convince Joel that he was wrong. Hell, he wished he could convince *himself* that Joel was wrong. Whether Kent wanted to admit it or not, Allison was the main reason his feelings for Christina had changed. Not that he was in love with Allison or anything. It wasn't that. It was just that Allison's return and his remembrance of the way he'd felt about her had simply emphasized to him that he didn't feel the same way about Christina. He sighed again. "You know," he said slowly, "maybe I should make a break with Christina."

"I agree," Joel said. "If you're no longer interested in her, you should."

Kent grimaced. "She's not going to like it."

"No, she probably won't."

"Do you have to agree with everything I say?"

Joel laughed. "Make up your mind. A few minutes ago you wanted me to agree with you."

"A real friend knows when to agree and when to disagree," Kent mumbled.

"He's just mad because it turned out I was right all the time," Joel said, grinning at Sam, the bartender, who stood a few feet away, not even trying to pretend he wasn't listening to their conversation.

Sam nodded sagely. "Some guys can't admit they made a mistake."

Kent stood, pulling a couple of dollars from his pocket and slapping them onto the bar. "That's it," he said. "I'm not going to sit here and be insulted. I'm going home."

Joel's laughter followed him out of the bar.

Allison wasn't sleeping well. Each night before going to bed she would tell herself she wasn't going to worry and she wasn't going to dream. Yet each night, as she lay in bed and waited for sleep to claim her, she worried. And after she finally fell asleep, she dreamed.

These dreams weren't erotic, as was the one she'd had about Kent. These dreams were filled with turmoil and left her shaken and troubled.

Over and over she relived the last weeks of her marriage to Jean Luc. They were weeks filled with bitter fights and hurtful words, weeks she wished she could wipe out of her mind forever, weeks she wished had never happened.

If only she could go back and live the weeks again, so that now when she did dream about her dead husband, the dreams would be poignant and sad, but wouldn't leave her riddled with guilt.

Especially painful was the last time she had seen Jean Luc alive. He had been packing to rejoin the racing circuit in Seville, and Allison, who had been looking for a good time to tell him about her pregnancy, decided to help him by refolding his shirts. She could see he had thrown them into his suitcase with no regard for how they would look when he unpacked them.

Jean Luc was shaving; she could see him through the partially opened bathroom door. Allison lifted the shirts out of the suitcase and laid them on the bed. One by one she neatly folded them and tucked them back into the suitcase.

Then she eyed his toiletries case, which was sitting open on the bed. She remembered that she'd purchased some of the English soap he liked so much the last time she'd gone shopping. She rummaged through the closet until she found the package. She removed one of the small, wrapped bars and put it into his toiletries case. As she withdrew her hand, a small plastic-wrapped package caught her eye.

She stared at it. Her heart began to pound in her chest as its meaning became clear to her.

Condoms.

Jean Luc had put a package of condoms in his toiletries case! Suddenly everything that was wrong in her marriage and her life erupted within. Breathing hard, she yanked the offensive packet from the toiletries case and charged into the bathroom. She pushed the door open so hard it hit Jean Luc in the back, and he cursed.

"What the devil—" Blood welled on his cheek where he had nicked himself.

"Just what were these doing in your toiletries case?" she demanded, shoving the packet under his nose. "Why would a married man need condoms on a trip where he won't be accompanied by his wife?" Her voice was shaking with fury.

Instead of apologizing or making up some excuse, Jean Luc raised his eyebrows in that infuriatingly superior way of his and said, "What I choose to pack is no business of yours."

"No business of mine!" Without thinking, she raised her hand and slapped him as hard as she could.

His blue eyes glittered with fury as he caught her right wrist in his strong hand. "Don't ever do that again," he said through gritted teeth, "or I won't be responsible for what happens to you."

"You—you...bastard!" Allison sputtered, so angry she couldn't find words to express how she felt. His casual dismissal of their marriage vows, his blatant disregard for her feelings, his refusal to even pretend he was sorry—all sickened her.

He continued to grip her wrist so hard it hurt, and the tendons of his bare arm stood out like ridges on a washboard. Voice full of contempt, he said, "Perhaps American women can call their husbands names and strike their husbands at will, but Frenchmen won't stand for such behavior. I suggest you go into the bedroom and calm yourself down."

Allison stared at him. She had known Jean Luc didn't love her the way she had once thought—hoped—he would. But this cold indifference, this total absence of feeling on his part, caused her heart to freeze. Suddenly all her fears were confirmed. Her marriage was a total sham.

To think she had been going to tell him her news. She had actually hoped that knowing they were going to have a child would make a difference to him, would magically heal her diseased marriage. Now she knew nothing would make a difference. Jean Luc didn't love her, and she didn't love him. Worse, he didn't respect her.

And she didn't respect him.

Allison's remaining innocence completely disappeared that day. She didn't answer Jean Luc, and after a moment he loosened his hold on her wrist. Allison rubbed it, then turned and, head held high, walked slowly out of the bathroom. She would not give him the satisfaction of running away. She walked out of the bedroom, down the hall and into the library, shutting the door behind her. She walked to the long casement window that overlooked the small park across from their apartment building. It was raining—a soft autumn rain—and through the wet glass she watched the people on the street below. Their colorful umbrellas bobbed as they walked along the leaf-strewn boulevard. Across the street, standing up against the wrought-iron fence that rimmed the park, a flower vendor—oblivious to the rain—hawked her wares.

As Allison stared out the window, she decided that when Jean Luc returned from Seville, she would tell him she wanted a divorce. She refused to consider what she would do if he said no.

An hour later he was gone. He never said goodbye. She heard the muffled noise that meant he had carried his bags into the foyer. She heard a low conversation between him and Madame Bergeron, their housekeeper. Then, minutes later, she heard the doorbell and, glancing down, saw a taxi stopped in front of the building.

She watched through the window as Jean Luc and the driver emerged, watched as they loaded Jean Luc's bags in the taxi, watched as Jean Luc climbed in the back and watched as the taxi sped away down the street.

Jean Luc didn't look back once.

After his taxi was no longer in sight, Allison walked back into their bedroom and, dry-eyed, looked around. She knew that she and Jean Luc would never share their canopied bed again. They would never be a couple again. Their marriage was over. She knew she should feel awful. Yet she didn't. All she felt right then was relief that she could finally admit to herself that she didn't care.

In fact, she hoped she'd never have to lay eyes on Jean Luc again.

Two days later she was notified of Jean Luc's death.

The sensible, rational part of her brain told her it wasn't her fault Jean Luc had been killed. But the other part—the emotional, irrational part—told her that maybe, just maybe, if she had told him about the baby, if they'd had a loving parting instead of a bitter one, if Jean Luc had known he was going to be a father—he would have been more careful.

And worst of all, if she hadn't wished never to see him again, maybe he would still be alive.

She knew she was being ridiculous. She knew she hadn't caused his race car to crash and burn. She knew his death wasn't her fault.

Still, she felt guilty. She felt guilty because she hadn't been able to love him the way she should have, and maybe that was why he couldn't be faithful to her. Perhaps he had sensed that her feelings weren't what they should be.

She had never told Jean Luc about Kent.

But she wondered if he'd known, anyway.

On the day of the race, had he been thinking about their fight? Was that why his concentration had slipped? Was that the reason he'd crashed? On and on her thoughts whirled with questions to which there were no answers.

Since then, no matter how many times she told herself none of it was her fault, a tiny part of Allison had always felt responsible for Jean Luc's death. Just as she now felt responsible for Marianne's problems.

So she hovered over Marianne, and the tension she felt transmitted itself to the baby, causing a negative effect. She cried more than normal, and even when sleeping, whimpered from time to time.

Allison knew this was bad for Marianne, but she felt powerless to change things. She just couldn't stop worrying. And nothing her father or Diana did to try to distract her worked.

Even the two visits Kent made to the house in the weeks after Marianne came home didn't seem to help because they were such impersonal visits. He dropped in. He asked about the baby. He was thoughtful and concerned about her welfare. But that was it. He and Allison were never alone together, and they made no progress toward establishing a more personal relationship.

She didn't think they ever would.

On Saturday afternoon, two weeks after Marianne had come home from the hospital, Allison, Lee and Diana were relaxing in the TV room when Kent stopped by on his way home from work. He walked into the middle of a discussion between Allison and her father—a discussion where Lee was urging her to get out more.

"What's the matter?" Kent asked.

"She's hovering over the baby too much," Lee explained. "She needs to get out of the house."

"I agree," Diana said gently. "It's not good for either you or Marianne to spend all your time with her. Why don't you call Marcy? Maybe go out to dinner and a movie?"

"No, really, I'm okay," Allison protested. She felt uncomfortable continuing this discussion in front of Kent.

"You're not okay," her father insisted. "All anyone has to do is look at you to see how stressed you are." He turned to Kent. "Don't you think so, Kent?"

Kent nodded thoughtfully. He seemed to consider a moment, then said, "Why don't I take you out to dinner tomorrow night?"

Both Allison and Diana stared at him. Lee grinned. "That's a great idea!" he said happily.

"You don't have to do that," Allison said. Her heart was thumping madly, and she wondered if she was blushing, because her face felt hot. Oh, Lord. What if Kent thought she had been maneuvering to get him to ask her out? She could have strangled her father.

"I know I don't have to," Kent said. He glanced at his mother, whose expression was noncommittal.

Allison thought she knew what Diana was thinking. "I can't leave Marianne," Allison said hurriedly.

"Of course you can," Lee said.

Finally Diana stirred herself. "Why can't you?" she asked. "Your father and I are here. Don't you trust us to watch her?"

Kent waited expectantly, and Allison wondered if pity was all that had prompted the invitation. She hoped he hadn't felt obligated to ask her, after what her father had said. What should she do? She desperately wanted to go. But part of her was afraid to. And it wasn't just fear of leaving Marianne, either. It was fear of the unknown. Fear of what would happen. Fear of what might be said. She swallowed nervously. "I...of course I trust you," she said to Diana. "I—"

"It's settled then," her father said. "You're going."

Allison's gaze met Kent's, and he smiled.

She knew she was lost.

* * *

All day Sunday Allison counted the minutes until seven-thirty, the time set for Kent to pick her up. Now she had something new to worry about.

What to wear.

She tried on outfit after outfit, discarding them mostly because nothing fit her properly any longer. Finally she settled on a forest green silk dress with a short, flared skirt, cap sleeves and a deep V neckline. With it she wore her thick gold necklace, a gold bangle bracelet and the heavy gold hoop earrings her Aunt Elizabeth had given her. And tonight, because it was a special night, she wore the large emerald ring her grandparents had given her for her eighteenth birthday.

She looked at herself in the mirror at least ten times, smoothing back her hair, touching up her makeup, wondering if her green eye shadow was too faint, then deciding it wasn't.

Finally seven-thirty came. After giving Marianne another kiss, she relinquished the baby to Diana's waiting arms, then walked slowly downstairs to meet Kent.

He stood in the wide foyer and watched her come down the stairs. He was wearing light gray dress slacks, a dark blue sport coat and a white shirt open at the collar. His dark hair was carefully brushed, and he looked casually elegant and so handsome he took her breath away.

When she reached floor level, he smiled down at her. "Hi."

Her silly heart decided to play leapfrog in her chest. "Hi," she said, knowing she sounded breathless and wishing she could be more casual and cool about this date. Stop thinking of it as a date, she told herself. You know why he invited you to dinner. He feels sorry for you. No more. No less.

Diana had walked downstairs, too, and held Marianne in her arms. Kent touched the baby's nose. "Hi, cutie," he said. "How're you feeling tonight?"

"She's had a good day today," Diana said.

Allison met Diana's gaze. "Now, if she should happen to—"

Diana interrupted her with a short laugh. "Allison, would you quit worrying? I know what to do."

"You know where Dr. Richardson's number is, don't you?" Allison persisted, already sorry she'd said she'd go tonight.

"Yes, I know where the doctor's number is." Diana rolled her eyes at Kent. "Would you get her out of here before she drives me crazy?"

With a laugh he took Allison's arm and steered her out the front door. The heat of the day still hovered in the air of the late-July evening. An army of cicadas sang as they walked to Kent's car, and the air was filled with the scent of newly mown grass. In the distance Allison heard the shouts of several children at play. Overhead, the sky had turned that hazy shade of lavender that signaled twilight, Allison's favorite time of day. She'd always thought that the world was a softer, more forgiving place at twilight, filled with a sense of peace that was missing at other times.

Her arm tingled where Kent's warm hand touched it, and when he opened the passenger door of the Corvette and helped her inside, she felt all shivery. So many memories came flooding back as he got into the car and she was surrounded by the scent of his after-shave, a subtle blend that reminded her of ocean breezes and warm sand. How many times had they been together like this in the intimate confines of a car?

"This is a nice car," she said as Kent turned the key in the ignition, put the Corvette in gear and began to back out of the driveway.

"Thanks. I like it."

"Um, where are we going?" she asked as she tried to quell her nervousness.

He shifted again, and the car shot forward. "I made reservations at Brennan's." There was an underlying tension in the casual admission. "I hope you don't mind."

"Why should I mind?" But she knew why. He had asked her to marry him after a dinner at Brennan's. She knew he was referring to that evening—remembering it, just as she was. "I love Brennan's," she added, wanting to dispel the sudden tension. Yet she wondered why he would purposely evoke it. Why pick Brennan's when there were so many other restaurants dotting the city? Did Kent want her to remember? She swallowed nervously. Oh, God. Why had she agreed to come tonight? What was going on?

They didn't talk much during the remainder of the drive downtown. Instead, Allison looked out her window and concentrated on relaxing. As usual, there were hundreds of joggers running in Memorial Park as the Corvette cruised down Memorial Drive. As they neared downtown, Allison admired the Houston skyline off to the right—an inky silhouette against the amethyst sky. She had always thought the city's skyline could hold its own against any city's, including some that were more renowned. She particularly enjoyed the modernistic twin peaks of the Pennzoil Building and the Dutch Renaissance look of the NCNB Building.

"Impressive, isn't it?" Kent said, breaking the silence.

"Yes."

"Glad you're back?"

Allison sighed. "Yes, I am. I just wish it were under happier circumstances." She wished she had nerve enough to ask him if he was glad she was back, too. Once she might have, but she had changed since that earlier, more self-assured time. Now she felt too uncertain of Kent's feelings and motives. Except for momentary flashes of emotion, he had given her no indication he was interested in anything except a family-type friendship between them.

Silence fell between them again, and Allison gazed out the window until they drew abreast of Brennan's.

"I see a parking place up the street," Kent said. "Do you mind walking? I don't trust these guys who valet park cars."

Allison grinned. Men were the same the world over when it came to their cars.

That quivery feeling of part excitement, part nervousness, returned as Kent helped her out of the car and kept his hand on her arm until they entered the restaurant. Another flood of memories engulfed Allison as she stood in the dimly lit entrance foyer and they waited to be seated. She glanced at the bowl of pralines sitting on the high table to their left, remembering how Kent had laughingly taken three of them as they exited the restaurant that night years ago.

"Kent!" she'd said, scandalized.

"What did I do?" he'd shot back, grinning with a little-boy innocent look that half exasperated, half enchanted her. "Nobody saw me," he whispered in her ear as they'd walked into the star-encrusted night.

Oh, I was such a fool to leave him.

"This way, please," the hostess said, breaking into Allison's poignant memory. She led them into the main dining room to her right.

Ten minutes later they were seated next to each other at a window table, overlooking the street. At least this was different, Allison thought in relief. The night they'd become engaged, they'd been seated at a window overlooking the inner courtyard.

For the next five minutes, Allison struggled to relax and deliberately avoided Kent's eyes. As the service people swirled around them, she wondered if Kent felt as uncomfortable as she did. She was grateful when their waiter came and took their drink order and gave them menus. That gave her something to look at, and she pretended to study the menu.

When their drinks arrived, Allison sipped at her wine, still avoiding Kent's gaze. She tried to think of something innocuous to say. She and Kent would never dispel the awkwardness between them completely. She'd been fooled into thinking they would because she'd grown comfortable around him at the house.

But this. This was different. This was old turf. Turf that stirred memories that should be kept buried. Memories that could do nothing but hurt her because they so sharply reminded her of what she'd lost.

"Allison?"

Slowly, reluctantly, Allison lifted her gaze and looked into Kent's eyes.

"This was a mistake, wasn't it?" he said.

Allison's heart went *thump, thump, thump*. She wet her lips.

"I shouldn't have brought you here. Do you want to leave?"

His eyes gleamed in the lamplight, never leaving her face. She shook her head. "No. I'm okay."

"Are you sure?"

"Yes." She would make sure she was okay. She would not embarrass herself or him. She was a woman of the world, wasn't she? She could handle this. She had handled much worse.

Still holding her gaze, he nodded. "Okay. But after dinner, I think we'd better talk."

"Talk?" Now her heart was going double-time: *thump-thump, thump-thump, thump-thump.*

"Yes. I think we've got some scores to settle, don't you?"

Chapter Seven

Scores to settle.

All through dinner, Allison thought about what Kent had said. She had known they would have to talk eventually. Just because she'd apologized didn't mean she was off the hook. Kent deserved a complete explanation of what had happened three and a half years ago, and she'd always known she'd have to give it to him.

It was going to be hard to talk about the past, but it really was best to get everything out in the open. That would be the only way they could possibly go forward.

She was almost relieved when dinner was over. She had hardly tasted her pasta-and-shrimp dish, even though Brennan's was famous for its Creole- and Cajun-inspired food.

Finally they were ready to leave. As they walked out together into the warm, humid night air, Kent said, "I know a little piano bar where it's pretty quiet and we can talk. Is that okay with you?''

''Yes, that's fine.''

Half an hour later they were seated across from each other in a dark booth. Allison had just called home and after being assured by Diana that Marianne was sleeping and doing fine, she had rejoined Kent. Now they looked at each other. Kent didn't say anything. Gathering her courage, Allison said, ''You're still angry with me, aren't you?''

He cupped his hands around his glass of Baileys liqueur and looked down. He shrugged. ''I'm trying not to be.''

''I know. And I appreciate that. But I feel your anger. And really... I—I guess I don't blame you. I know I hurt you. But, you know, Kent, I'm not sure I'm solely to blame for what happened.''

His gaze slowly met hers.

Before she lost her nerve, she plunged on. ''I've thought about this a lot. I know I was selfish and self-centered, and I know I was a fool to have run off like that, but I think there was a basic problem between us that had nothing to do with what kind of job you accepted.''

Now she really had his attention. She could see it in the way he sat a little taller and in the way his eyes had locked with hers.

''What kind of basic problem?'' he said.

''I don't think we ever really listened to each other.''

He seemed to consider her statement for a moment, then said slowly, ''Would you explain that?''

''Well, think about it. You were talking. I was talking. But did we really hear what the other one was saying?''

He shrugged. "Maybe not." He twirled his glass in his hands, and Allison's gaze was drawn to them. She admired the way they looked—strong and solid, with long fingers and neatly trimmed nails. She thought about all the times those hands had touched her. And all the ways. Casually. And not so casually. She remembered how good they'd felt, how much she'd welcomed his touch. As the memories flooded her, she wished . . . no. There was no sense wishing. What was past was past. They couldn't go back in time.

"You hurt me, you know," he said, still rotating the glass. "I was a real mess after you left." His direct gaze held hers, and his hands stilled.

The moment trembled between them. There was so much to say. So much pain to heal. So much to atone for. Allison's chest felt tight as the weight of the past pressed down on her. Striving for calm, she murmured, "I was a real mess, too."

"Why?" he said, urgency and bewilderment in his voice. "Why did you just take off like that? Why wouldn't you talk to me? I tried to see you, you know."

"I know." Allison was fighting tears. She took a deep breath, hoping it was too dark in the bar for Kent to know how close she was to breaking down. She mustn't break down. She mustn't.

"Your grandmother said you didn't want to talk to me." All the bitterness and pain he must have felt at the time pulsed in his voice.

She had been staying with her grandparents at the time of their breakup. She remembered that awful morning. "I didn't."

"But why not? I've never understood that." His gaze pinned hers.

He had such honest eyes. They demanded a corresponding honesty from her. "I—I think I was afraid to see you."

"Afraid of *me?*"

"No, no, not afraid of you! Afraid of my own weakness as far as you were concerned."

"I don't understand."

"I'm not sure I do, either." How could she explain her flawed reasoning? She'd mulled it all over so many times, and she still wasn't sure she understood it completely. Trying to formulate her answer, she sipped at her Kahlúa.

Finally she said, "It's complicated, but I've thought about this a lot. I was so set in my idea of the way our life would be. I pictured you working for Keating & Shaw...making lots of money."

She spoke slowly, thoughtfully. This was so important. She had to try to make him understand the way her brain had worked. "I had it all worked out. I pictured myself coming to watch you work in court. Meeting you downtown for lunch. I saw us living in a beautiful house, with me giving elegant dinner parties. I could just see all of our friends...your associates and their wives...coming and going. The two of us getting written up in B. J. Barrette's column."

Kent's face twisted in the semblance of a smile.

She sighed. "You know...up-and-coming young lawyer and his wife. I had it all planned. The perfect marriage. The total package." Allison bit her lip. "I had been prepared for a life like the one I've described all of my life. And when you talked about opening the storefront office, I just couldn't see it. I thought...I don't know what I thought."

Their gazes met and held. She closed her eyes briefly, then opened them again. His eyes hadn't wavered. Be honest, she reminded herself. "Okay. I do know what I thought. I thought you'd change your mind."

He looked at her for a long time. Piano music and the muted conversations of the other patrons of the bar surrounded them. Finally he spoke. "And I thought you'd change yours."

"Yes! That's what I've been trying to tell you. Neither of us was really listening. I couldn't see your vision. And I know now that you couldn't see mine. Anyway, I didn't want to give up that picture in my mind. I didn't want to concede, in any way, that you might be right to follow your dream. I didn't want to compromise. So I closed my eyes to reality...." She laughed without mirth. "Isn't that funny? I'd accused you of being a romantic and prided myself on my realism, and there I was, completely ignoring reality and indulging my own foolish, romantic dreams."

"Allison—"

"No. Let me finish. I kept telling myself you would see the error of your ways. That if you really loved me, you'd take the job with Keating & Shaw." Again, she met his gaze squarely. "And then, when I went to Paris, I told myself that if you *really* cared, you'd come after me."

What was he thinking? she wondered as her words flowed between them, pulsing in the air like static electricity.

"I thought about coming after you."

The quiet admission caused her heart to leap. "You did?"

He nodded. "But I guess pride kept me away. I told myself you didn't really love me if you could throw away what we had so easily."

Pride.

Yes, she thought. Pride got in my way, too. She had taken a stand and couldn't back down. Oh, God. What a mess we made of things. We hurt each other so much. And for what?

"Kent," she said haltingly, "there's something I have to ask you."

"Ask away."

"Why did you give up your storefront practice?"

He grimaced. "It's ironic, really. It didn't take long for me to realize your father was right all along."

"What do you mean?"

"Once he told me that I had some kind of romantic dream of being a modern-day Don Quixote. And he was right. I did. You say you had a picture in your mind. Well, I did, too. Only my picture was very different from yours. I saw myself as the champion of the downtrodden. Riding in on a white horse and taking on all comers. Defending innocent people who couldn't afford high-priced lawyers. Going up against the establishment and winning. Truth and honor besting the big guys." He laughed, the sound derisive and cynical. "Talk about being naive! Jesus, it's no wonder I got shot down!"

It hurt her to hear him. For so long she had comforted herself with the thought that his dream had come true. She didn't want to know that even when your intentions were completely unselfish, things could sometimes go wrong. Right didn't always come out on top. "What happened?"

He shook his head, then drained his glass of Baileys. "Well, my disenchantment with the storefront wasn't sudden. It came gradually...over a period of two years. I don't know. I got so tired of plea bargains and deals. Drugs and poverty. It all began to seem so hopeless to me. As if no matter what I did, nothing would ever change. You know, gridlock is the name of the game. And then came the straw that broke the camel's back."

Allison waited quietly.

"I took on this case. A young girl named Jessie. She'd been accused of selling crack. She was a single mother, two small kids. She brought the kids with her when she came to see me. They looked so pathetic with their big eyes and scared faces. Jessie pleaded with me. 'I'm innocent,' she said. 'I can't go to jail. Who'll watch my kids?' The kids were clinging to her hands, looking at me. And Jessie—" he made a sound of disgust, a cross between a laugh and a snort "—you should have seen her. She looked like a kid herself. Hell, she is a kid. She was a mother at fourteen. Even now she's only twenty-one. Well, anyway, the police had no real evidence against her. Everything they had was circumstantial. Damned incriminating, but still circumstantial. Anyway, to make a long story short, I got her off. Afterward I found out she really *had* been selling crack. In fact, I found out she had no intention of stopping. She bragged about it. Was proud of how she'd fooled everyone, including me."

His gaze met Allison's again. "When I found out that I'd worked my tail off for a woman who didn't give a damn about her kids or anything but selling enough crack to keep herself supplied, I just lost it. I couldn't believe it. I'd put everything—heart and soul—into defending her. I'd believed her. Believed in her. And all the time she'd been lying to me. I mean, who needed it? I finally wised up. If I was gonna bust my ass, I might as well be making money while I was doing it.''

Allison wanted to reach out and take his hands in hers. Even when she'd berated him for his idealism, that quality was one of the reasons she'd loved him so much. Why didn't I realize it before? she asked herself. "So you went to work for Keating & Shaw after all.''

"Yep. Like I said, I finally wised up.''

"Do you like working for them?''

"Yeah, I like it fine,'' he said quickly. Too quickly, she thought. "Of course, I've had to readjust my thinking.''

"In what way?''

"Well, now I'm on the side of the big guys usually.''

"And how do you feel about that?''

"I feel fine about it. Why shouldn't I? I'm doing what a lawyer is supposed to do—protecting my client's interests. That's what they pay me to do.''

Allison nodded, but she heard the note of defensiveness in his voice. "What kinds of cases have you worked on?'' Somehow she just couldn't picture Kent getting fired up about defending big oil companies or the like.

"All kinds. Right now I'm assigned to a personal-injury case against one of our biggest clients.''

"Tell me about it.''

"Are you really interested?''

"Yes, I am.'' She needed to know. She needed to see if her instincts were right, if he was just pretending to be happy.

Allison listened carefully as he told her about Emmett Wilder and the suit that had been brought against him. She listened not just to Kent's words, but to all the nuances of his tone and all the things she imagined he wasn't saying.

"Anyway," Kent finished, "we're still in the process of discovery, so right now I'm going over all the records relating to the design of the bike and preparing to interview the members of the design team. We don't want any surprises in court."

"I'm assuming there was a flaw in the design of the bike."

"Yes. That's why Petrowski crashed."

"Do you think Wilder knew about the flaw?"

"He says he didn't."

"What if he *was* guilty? Could you still defend him?"

"Well, he's not, so the question isn't relevant."

"But just for the sake of argument, what if he was?"

"It's my job to give my client the best possible defense. No more. No less."

"Guilty or not?"

"Guilty or not."

Allison stared at him. "That—that doesn't sound like you."

"What doesn't sound like me?"

"I—I just never imagined you could feel that way. That you could defend someone, guilty or not."

"Allison, that's what a lawyer does." He laughed, a short, harsh sound. "What did you think when you were urging me to go to work for Keating & Shaw? That I'd be defending little old ladies who got hit by trucks? The truth is, most lawyers are defending big companies who want to keep their losses at a minimum."

"But Kent...how can you feel good about defending someone who is making money off someone else's misery?"

"Hey, if it weren't for misery, there'd be no lawyers!"

Allison couldn't prevent what she knew was a stricken look from crossing her face.

"Oh, hell," he said with a sigh. "That's just an old, tired joke. I was only kidding. Don't look like that."

Allison hated the cynicism she heard in his voice. This was not the old Kent. This was not the Kent who could no more defend a guilty man than he could torture an animal. She wasn't sure she even knew this Kent. It was going to be very hard for her to accept the changes in him. From white knight in blue jeans to a take-the-money-and-run guy in an expensive suit. Surely, buried deep beneath this new, hard shell was the Kent she had known and loved—the compassionate, warm, caring man who wanted to save the world. She had to believe this was true. She *did* believe this was true.

People have let him down. Too many people, including me. That's why he pretends not to care. He cares. He's just put up walls to protect himself. Slowly the hope grew that maybe, since she'd been one of the ones who'd been responsible for the walls, she could be a major catalyst in bringing the walls down again.

"So now that I've told you about me, why don't we talk about you?" he said.

Allison had been afraid the conversation would get around to her. But fair was fair. He deserved his turn. "What do you want to know?"

"Why did you marry Fornier? Did you love him?"

Allison bowed her head so she didn't have to see his eyes. Now was the moment of truth. "I thought I did." When Kent didn't answer, she looked up. "I married him on the rebound."

He nodded slowly.

"It—it wasn't a very happy marriage. And I blame myself for that."

"Do you want to talk about it?"

She shook her head. "No. It's over with. I made a mistake, but Jean Luc is dead, so there's really no sense in dredging it all up again." She knew he deserved more than this inadequate explanation, but she just couldn't talk about her marriage tonight. Maybe after Marianne's surgery. After the baby was well. After Allison no longer felt so guilty. Maybe then she'd be ready to open herself up and let Kent see all her scars.

Keeping her face carefully blank, she picked up her purse from the seat beside her. "It's getting late, Kent. I should be getting home. I don't want to leave Marianne too long." She knew if she brought Marianne's name into the conversation, Kent would give her no argument.

"Okay, sure."

As they walked out into the velvety night air, Kent said, "I'm glad we talked."

Allison drew a deep breath. "Yes. Me, too." But they weren't through talking. She knew it. And she knew he knew it, too.

Kent drove slowly. He didn't want the evening to end. Tonight, for the first time since Allison's return, he felt almost relaxed in her company. He was very glad they had made a beginning at clearing the air. He still wasn't sure he understood her reasons for running away the way she had, but at least they were talking to each other again. Really talking.

Allison had changed, he thought as he glanced at her profile. She had matured. She had left Houston a girl; now she was a woman. He guessed that wasn't surprising after all she'd been through. He liked her new maturity. Wistfully he wondered if things would have been different if they'd met now instead of years ago.

As if she sensed his look, she turned, smiling slightly. He'd inserted a CD by Harry Connick, Jr., and the mellow jazz floated in the air between them. He smiled back.

It was nice having her here in his car. Like old times. He smiled wryly. Well, not exactly like old times. When they'd been engaged, she had usually insisted that he drive her little sports car—a present from her Marlowe grandparents—instead of his battered old Honda. He guessed if he'd been thinking with his brains instead of his hormones, he'd have realized that Allison would never be contented with anything but the best.

Even the ring he'd given her had symbolized the differences between them. He had intended to give her a small but tasteful diamond, but the look on her face when she'd seen the array of modest stones had changed his mind for him. And fast. He'd ended by buying her a one-and-a-half-carat ring that he could ill afford. In fact, he'd used a large portion of his seed money for the storefront, which meant he'd had to start up his business with much less capital than he'd hoped.

He still had that ring. He'd intended to take it back, knowing Sedgewick Mason, the jeweler who'd sold it to him, would have given him a full refund. Sedgewick was a friend of his mother's. But somehow he never had. He wondered what Allison would say if she knew. She would probably be astounded at his sentimentality. Maybe not, though. After all, as she'd pointed out, she had once accused him of being a hopeless romantic, whereas she prided herself on her more pragmatic approach to life.

His thoughts continued in this vein until he turned onto the street where Lee's home was located. It wasn't very late, but most of the large homes, which sat far back on the wooded lots, were dark. Kent pulled into the long driveway and stopped just outside the gate. Lee had purchased the house before he and Diana married, and he'd once told Kent he especially liked its location—at the curve of a cul-de-sac that backed up to Buffalo Bayou.

Kent helped Allison out of the car, and after unlocking the gate, they walked together into the walled courtyard and up to the double walnut doors. The two lamps mounted on either side of the massive doors bathed them in pools of gold as they stopped under their soft glow.

The heavy scent of summer roses filled the air, and through the tall pine trees that dotted the grounds, a full moon spilled pearls of light. In the woods bordering the bayou, Kent could hear the rustle of small feet—probably chipmunks or squirrels, he thought, although once his mother had come face-to-face with a skunk at the back of their property. He chuckled, remembering Lee's laughing description of Diana's shriek and headlong flight into his arms.

"What are you grinning about?" Allison asked.

"Oh, just remembering when my mother saw a skunk out here."

"Out here!" She moved instinctively closer, looking around in obvious alarm.

He laughed again, but he felt a warm pleasure at her basic assumption that he would protect her. Without thinking, he placed his hands on her shoulders, feeling the warm, firm flesh under the thin silk of her dress.

Suddenly a sizzling awareness arched between them, and Allison slowly raised her head.

In the golden light her eyes shone like polished stone. Her scent, something fresh and light as raindrops, drifted around him. Her face, partly in shadow, partly illuminated, looked so familiar and so achingly lovely. Her mouth—a mouth that had always begged to be kissed, with its full, sensuous lips—was slightly open, waiting. Inviting. Tempting.

His hands tightened on her shoulders, and he felt her tremble.

He wanted to kiss her.

He knew he shouldn't.

He knew nothing would be solved or changed or worked out by giving in to this powerful physical attraction he still felt for her.

He also knew she wanted him to kiss her.

He lowered his head, and the moment his lips met hers, the moment he tasted the unique essence that was Allison, he was lost. He folded her into his arms and kissed her as if there would be no tomorrow. He kissed her like a dying man who was eating his last meal and intended to extract the last drop of satisfaction and enjoyment from it. He kissed her as if he would never have a chance to kiss her again.

And she kissed him back. She never resisted him at all. She wound her arms around his neck and welcomed him. She gave herself so sweetly and so thoroughly that his blood pounded through his veins and his heart galloped in his chest and his entire body felt dazed and drugged and discombobulated.

They clung to each other, and he could feel the soft curves of her body aligned against his and his body's corresponding reaction. His hands roamed her back, then dropped to cup her rounded bottom and pull her tightly against him so she could feel how much he wanted her.

He might never have pulled away. He might have continued kissing her and touching her until there was no question of stopping. But when he forced her awareness of his arousal, she abruptly pulled away. She was breathing hard, and Kent felt as if he'd been hit by a train.

"Kent, I—I don't think we should do this."

Still stunned and shaken by feelings he'd thought he'd put behind him, he said stiffly, "I guess I misunderstood. It won't happen again."

"Please, Kent, don't be angry. I—I just need some time. I'm too confused about everything and too worried about Marianne. I can't handle anything else right now."

Kent knew she was right. He wanted to stay aloof. Act as if he couldn't care less that she had withdrawn. Again. But he heard the genuine misery in her voice. And he knew she was being honest with him. Sighing with regret, he kissed her cheek gently, resisting the impulse to run his lips over its petal-soft surface. "You're right, of course," he said. "I was out of line."

"No! I don't want you to think that. You weren't out of line. I—I wanted you to kiss me. But...everything is happening too fast. I need time to think. And I think you do, too."

Chapter Eight

Allison lay awake a long time. She relived every moment of her evening with Kent, especially the kiss he'd given her and the strength of her reaction to it.

She had never dreamed she would feel that way again. She had never imagined that Kent—with one plundering kiss—would unleash all those needs and desires that had lain so long unfulfilled. She had never believed that the physical attraction she'd always felt for Kent could be so easily rekindled.

One kiss.

One stunning, earth-moving kiss.

She almost laughed. Would have laughed if there'd been anything to laugh about.

She still loved him. And she still wanted him. But giving in to this want, to this love, would be madness. Because even though they'd made a beginning tonight, they had not worked out all the old problems. There was still a lot of hurtful stuff between them. And until they understood it and could overcome it, starting a physical relationship would only complicate matters.

And Allison did not need another complication in her life. Marianne and her physical problems were complication enough. Marianne had to be Allison's only consideration right now. Allison and Kent and their troubled past and uncertain future could drain none of Allison's needed energy.

So, regretfully, as much as Allison might want to explore whether she and Kent could ever regain what they'd lost, she knew she'd been right to call a halt tonight. She simply couldn't take on a highly charged emotional involvement. For now, anyway, they had to cool it. She resolved to tell Kent her decision the next time she saw him.

But right before she fell asleep, she admitted to herself that it was going to be hard—very hard—to keep to her good resolutions.

When Kent arrived home after his dinner date with Allison, he saw the message light blinking on his answering machine. He pressed the Play button, then began to undress.

"Damn you, Kent! Where are you?" Christina's angry voice filled the room. "Did you forget we were using the Astros' tickets tonight?"

Kent stopped in the process of unbuttoning his shirt. Holy sh— He broke off the thought as Christina's tirade continued unabated. After a string of curses he'd never heard her use before, he heard the click as she hung up. He sank into the nearest chair and closed his eyes. He couldn't believe it, but he had completely forgotten he and Christina had made plans to use the firm's box seats for tonight's Astros game. He hadn't seen her all day yesterday, and she hadn't reminded him on Friday. But that was no excuse. They had talked about it earlier in the week. He couldn't imagine how he could have forgotten.

Oh, boy. He was really going to get a piece of her mind tomorrow. He wasn't looking forward to it. And he could just imagine what she'd say if she knew he had taken Allison out instead.

He opened his eyes, staring sightlessly at the far wall. He couldn't tell her. He would have to lie. But should he lie? Only pond scum lied about something like that. Wouldn't it be better to be honest? Take his lumps? He'd been thinking he should break off with Christina, anyway, and wasn't this the perfect time to do it? She could yell at him, call him names and save face. She could break off with him, instead of vice versa.

Or maybe not. Maybe he should tell part of the truth but not let her know who his date was.

He was still trying to decide which approach was best when he finally fell asleep hours later.

"Where the hell were you?" were the first words Christina said on Monday morning. Her voice was tight and controlled, barely a whisper, because they were standing in the hall outside the conference room, surrounded by dozens of their associates. They were all waiting for the Monday-morning meeting to start.

"I'll tell you later," he said. "I'm really sorry," he added.

She wasn't moved by his apology. She narrowed her eyes and glared at him.

All during the meeting, he could feel her watching him.

Later, in the privacy of his small office where she'd followed him after the meeting, she faced him. "Well?"

He wet his lips. "I . . . uh . . ." He took a deep breath. "Look, I feel like a real jerk, but I forgot."

"You forgot," she said through gritted teeth. Her gray eyes looked like slate—hard and flat and cold. Her chest was heaving under her royal blue suit coat. "You forgot," she repeated.

He nodded. "I'm sorry," he said again.

"Where were you?"

"I'd gone out to dinner."

"Alone?"

This was the moment of truth. "No. I had a date."

Two bright red spots of color appeared on her cheeks. "You had a date," she said softly. "You forgot about me and made another date."

Kent cringed. "Yes." Whatever she said or chose to do, he deserved it.

She stared at him for what seemed like hours, but in reality was probably only a minute. Kent met her stare and waited. "Nobody treats me like this," she said, her voice shaking. "It's that ex-fiancée of yours, isn't it? I knew the moment I saw her she was bad news!" Her eyes narrowed. "The only thing I've got to say to you, Kent, is that you're going to be sorry. Very sorry!"

And then she stalked out of his office.

All day long Kent fought the urge to call Allison. After he finally stopped thinking about Christina and how justifiably angry she had been, he began to relive the previous evening, especially the heated kiss he and Allison had shared.

He had kissed a lot of women since Allison left him years ago. None had made him feel the way he'd felt last night. Oh, he'd been turned on by some of the kisses. Physically turned on. But no one except Allison had ever had the power to turn him on emotionally.

That knowledge scared the stuffing out of him. Because that meant he was not over Allison. That meant she still had control over him. Once before, he'd let her control him, and it hadn't worked out. And it had hurt like hell when she'd ditched him. Did he really want to let himself be in a position for her to hurt him again?

Did he have a choice?

You always have a choice.

All day, in between phone calls and reading and dictating, his thoughts were threaded with bits and pieces of the previous evening.

He was still thinking about Allison when, late in the afternoon, he got a call from Marcy Bartlett, Joel's wife.

"Hi, Marce! How are you?"

"I'm fine. How're you doing?"

"Great. Just great."

"Listen, Kent, Joel and I are having a small dinner party Friday night. We'd like you to come."

"What!" he said in mock indignation. "Is Joel reneging on our standing date for a beer after work?"

"Yes," Marcy said with a laugh. "Under protest, of course. But seriously, can you come?"

"Who else is coming?"

"Well..." She hesitated just long enough for Kent to realize she was up to something. "Oh, fiddle. You'll find out anyway. I've invited Allison."

He smiled. Matchmaking. Marcy was matchmaking.

"You'll come, won't you, Kent?"

Oh, hell, he wanted to go. "Yes, sure. I'll come."

"And Kent?"

"Yeah?"

"It might be nice if you gave Allison a ride."

Allison hoped she looked all right. She didn't know what was wrong with her that she was so undecided about what to wear lately. Normally she felt confident of her clothes sense and her judgment. But now, where Kent was concerned, she was suddenly all indecisive and girlish.

She'd chosen a soft pants outfit in a creamy, soft fabric with matching bone-colored flats and gold jewelry. It was, after all, just a dinner at Marcy and Joel's.

Nervously Allison waited for Kent's arrival. When he'd called earlier in the week to ask if he could pick her up and take her to the dinner, at first she'd said, "Maybe it would be best for us to go separately." But she hated driving alone at night, and after all, there was no harm in accepting a ride, was there? It wasn't as if she were going to go to bed with him or anything.

"You look nice," Diana said when Allison walked into the living room a few minutes later.

"Thanks."

"Would you like a glass of wine, honey?" her father asked. He and Diana sat opposite each other on matching love seats. Diana had a glass of wine in her hand, and Lee was drinking something from an on-the-rocks glass. A plate of pâté and crackers sat on the coffee table between them.

"No, I don't think so. Kent should be here any minute."

The words were no sooner out of her mouth than she heard the clunk of a car door outside. Her stomach fluttered as Diana said, "I think I hear him now."

A few seconds later the doorbell rang, and Allison, nervously smoothing down her pants, walked out to the foyer. Her heart skidded up into her throat as she opened the door and Kent smiled down upon her.

"Hi," he said, giving her an admiring glance.

"Hi." Would the sight of him always make her feel this way? She wondered if long-married couples still felt this giddy sensation when the object of their affections came into sight. God, she hoped not. She couldn't imagine how anyone could stand this constant state of edginess, this perpetual nervousness. She felt unhinged, and she wasn't sure she liked the feeling.

"Where are the old folks?" Kent said with a conspiratorial wink.

Allison grinned, and her stomach settled down a bit. "They're in the living room."

"Guess I'd better pay my respects."

"I heard you call us 'old folks,'" Diana said when Kent and Allison entered the living room. She raised her face as Kent leaned down to hug her and kiss her cheek. Lee stood, and the two men shook hands.

"Do you have time for a drink before you go?" Lee asked.

Kent shook his head. "Better not. Marcy said dinner at seven-thirty." He glanced at the mantel clock. "And it's already after seven."

A few minutes later they left. As they drove down the curving street leading to lower Memorial Drive, the sun was lowering in the west, and the world was bathed in amber and scarlet. Allison's tension had returned now that she and Kent were alone again, and she concentrated on taking even breaths to try to dispel it. She wondered if Kent felt the same way. The silence between them was beginning to be uncomfortable. To combat it, she said, "Tonight should be fun, don't you think?"

Kent smiled, giving her a brief look, then turning his attention back to the road.

Wasn't he going to help her out at all? Why didn't he say something? "Marcy said she'd also invited Gail and Michael Berry." When Allison and Kent were engaged, Gail and Michael had rounded out their group of special friends. Michael, like Joel and Kent, was a lawyer, and Gail, an artist, worked for a big ad agency.

"I know."

"Do—do you see them often?"

"Not as often as I'd like." There was an odd note in his voice.

What did that odd note mean? "I guess you're all too busy," Allison offered.

"It's not that. It's..." He hesitated, drumming his fingers against the steering wheel. They were stopped for the light where Memorial Drive met the Loop. "Well, they're married, and I'm not."

Allison didn't answer. She knew he was thinking exactly what she was thinking. We could have been married. We could have been a part of this special group for years now. Another thought, one Allison had had many times, followed naturally. Marianne could have been Kent's baby. Our baby. Once more the heartache that always seemed to be hovering just under the surface rushed through her. Who knows? Maybe Marianne wouldn't have been born with a problem if she had been Allison and Kent's child. Oh, God. She had to stop thinking these black thoughts. They helped no one. They accomplished nothing except making her feel worse about herself and her poor judgment than she already did.

A silence fell between them again, and in the ten or so minutes it took to reach Marcy and Joel's West University home, Allison struggled to regain her composure.

When they arrived at the Bartletts', they pulled into the driveway and parked behind a dark green Jaguar. "The Berrys are here," Kent said.

"I can see he's doing well, too," Allison commented as she eyed the Jaguar.

Kent, who had just turned off the ignition, looked at her. His brow was furrowed. "We work damned hard for our money," he said.

Oh-oh. There was a definite note of defensiveness in his voice. "I know," she said hurriedly. "I didn't mean to suggest you didn't." She made a mental note to be careful. Kent was obviously sensitive to remarks about how much money he made. She saw his sensitivity as another clue that he wasn't entirely comfortable with the way he was making his living, no matter what he said.

She was very grateful they had arrived at their destination. Once they were inside the Bartletts' home and surrounded by their friends, Allison felt herself relaxing. She could see Kent was more comfortable, too.

"It's so good to have you home again, Allison," Gail Berry said, giving Allison a smile.

"I'm glad to be here, believe me." She smiled at Gail, a classy-looking brunette who wore huge round glasses with bright red frames and was given to dressing in flowing skirts and dresses in vivid primary colors matched with long, trailing scarves.

The three women were sipping at a predinner cocktail in Marcy's living room. The men had disappeared into Joel's study, where he was presumably showing off his new computer.

"Are you and Kent an item again?" Gail asked, her dark eyes bright with curiosity.

Allison looked at Marcy. "No, but I think Marcy wishes we would be."

Marcy grinned sheepishly. "I admit it. I'd love to see them get back together." She leaned forward and said in a conspiratorial whisper, "I think he's still in love with you."

Allison could feel her face warming up. To cover her confusion, she lifted her glass to her lips and sipped. "We're just friends," she said, but she could feel her heart beating too fast. Despite what Marcy hoped, Allison knew her decision to keep her relationship with Kent one of friendship only was the right one.

Gail and Marcy exchanged a coy look.

Allison was saved from having to say anything more by the reappearance of the men. They were laughing as they walked into the room, and Allison looked up. The thought flashed through her mind that of the three of them, Kent stood out. It wasn't just that he was better looking than either Joel, who was smaller and more serious looking, or Michael, who was short and a little overweight. Kent had more presence. There was a quality about him that was hard to define, but Allison knew that anyone looking at him would know he was a bright and shining star who would make his mark on the world.

Pride swelled her heart as she looked at him. For one crystal moment their gazes met and clung. Then Joel, laughing, said something, and the moment was gone.

* * *

"Allison, you're awfully quiet tonight," Michael said about halfway through dinner. He was seated on her right, Joel on her left. Kent was diagonally across the table.

"Am I? I'm sorry." She had been dreaming about the past again, imagining what her life would be like if she and Kent were now married, as their friends were.

"She's got a lot on her mind," Marcy said.

Michael nodded. "Yes, Gail told me about your baby."

"I was hoping you'd bring her tonight," Gail said.

"It's best not to take her out unless I absolutely have to. She's supposed to be kept as quiet as possible," Allison explained.

"I'm dying to see her," Gail said.

"You're welcome to come over anytime," Allison said.

Gradually the conversation drifted to other things, but the mention of Marianne and her problems was a reminder of what Allison had decided earlier.

She was going to cool it with Kent.

And she would tell him so on the way home.

Chapter Nine

Some things were easier said than done.

Three times on the way home Allison had tried to introduce the subject of their relationship. She would open her mouth, all set to say what she had been thinking, then she would lose her nerve. The trouble was, when she was around Kent, all she could think about was how she felt about him.

No. Be honest, she told herself. The real trouble was, down deep she didn't want to cool it with Kent.

It was that kiss. If only she could wipe that kiss out of her mind. Too many times tonight, as she'd looked at Kent's mouth or his hands, she'd remember that kiss.

She wondered if he had thought about the kiss, too. Had it meant anything to him at all? Had there been any of the emotions she was feeling behind the kiss? Or with Kent, was it just that same potent physical attraction they'd always felt for one another? With the old Kent, she would have known what he was feeling. But this new Kent was another story. Maybe he kissed everyone the way he'd kissed her.

Like that blonde. She wondered if he was still seeing Christina. Kissing her the way he'd kissed Allison. Envy knifed through her and with it a feeling close to despair because she knew she had no right to be envious. Kent was free to kiss whomever he pleased, whenever he pleased. He was also free to make love to anyone at all. Allison had no claims on him. *So what are you waiting for? Why don't you get it over with? Tell him what you decided about cooling it.*

She stared out the passenger-side window as the music from a Paula Abdul CD played softly. Why did life have to hurt so much? Why was everything so... hard? For a moment she wished she were eighteen again, when her biggest problem was what color dress to wear for graduation. Wouldn't it be wonderful if she could do everything all over? And this time she'd do it all right.

But then, if she were eighteen again, she wouldn't have Marianne. She sighed deeply, closing her eyes against the night lights of the city. No. She didn't want to be eighteen again. She wouldn't trade Marianne for anything.

"That was a big sigh," Kent said.

Allison opened her eyes and turned toward him. She tried to smile, but a smile just wouldn't come. Once again tears hovered just beneath the surface. Oh, she was sick of feeling so weepy!

"Is something wrong?" he asked. "Didn't you have a good time tonight?"

"I had a great time tonight. And, no, nothing's wrong." Quit acting like a wimp, she told herself. And for the rest of the ride home, she forced herself to talk about the evening. Kent told her a couple of stories about Michael and Joel, and Allison even found herself laughing.

But as they pulled into the driveway at her father's house, all her earlier tension returned. What if Kent tried to kiss her again tonight? What would she do? You should have told him your decision on the way home, she scolded herself.

When Kent came around to her side of the car and helped her out of the Corvette, just the simple touch of his hand on her arm sent all kinds of messages to her brain—messages that Allison did not welcome because she knew they would only make things more difficult for her. But she was powerless to stop them. Powerless to stop the shivery awareness. Powerless to stop the aching need that rippled through her as Kent walked her to the door.

Tell him. Tell him.

They were standing in the courtyard once again. Like a replay of the previous weekend. Allison looked up. "Kent, I—"

The words died on her lips as he reached out and took her hand in his. The simple contact set her heart to pounding. "Listen, Allison," he said. "All week I've been thinking about what you said last Sunday night, and you're right. Anything but friendship between us would be a big mistake." He hesitated, and his words hung in the air between them. "Just as it was last time."

Something hard knotted in Allison's chest, and she pulled her hand away. She knew he was only reinforcing what she herself had said. And she knew he was right. She had been planning to say exactly the same thing. So why did the words hurt so much?

Somehow she managed to keep her voice steady as she said, "I'm glad you see it that way. Well, thanks for the ride. I enjoyed the evening." It took everything she had, every ounce of strength, to smile, but she did it. "Good-night, Kent." Then, before he could say more than a soft good-night in return, she turned and inserted her key into the lock, opening the door quickly.

Then she walked inside and shut the door behind her.

Kent spent a hellish weekend. Ever since Allison's return, nothing had gone right in his life. He'd alienated Christina, and now, for some stupid reason, he felt as if he'd done something wrong with Allison, too. He kept replaying his conversation with her on Friday night after Marcy and Joel's party. Why had he gotten the impression that he'd said something he shouldn't have said?

By Monday morning he decided he was not going to think about women at all. Period. He was swearing off all women—at least for the duration of the Wilder case. He'd been neglecting his work because of his entanglements, and that would have to stop. It would stop.

Determined and purposeful, he went to the office early and began the laborious task of reading his share of the R & D notes on the Wild Rider.

Late Monday afternoon, while looking through the last notebook, Kent abruptly stopped reading. He stared at a notation about a third of the way down the page. That couldn't be right. He blinked twice, then focused on the line he'd just read. He read it again: CONT TO CK W.R. F/PRBLM W/STRG. AB.

Kent read the cryptic message aloud. He'd looked at so many pages of notes that he pretty much understood the shorthand used by the design team. He began to translate. "Continuing to check Wild Rider for problem with..." With what? The steering?

Chilled, he looked at the date again—the previous November. One month before the Wild Rider was test ridden by Greg Petrowski. One month before the steering mechanism had failed and Petrowski had been killed.

Continuing to check?

The note was initialed "AB." Armand Brasselli, the head of the design team. The man Kent's secretary had been trying get an appointment with so that Kent could interview him, but who, so far, she'd had no success in reaching.

That phrase, *continuing to check*, really troubled Kent, because according to Emmett Wilder, there had been no problem at all in the preliminary testing of the steering. So why would the designer be *continuing* to check something with which they did not have a problem to begin with?

Kent frowned and swiveled his chair so he could prop his feet on his wastebasket. Had Armand Brasselli made other notes about the steering? Earlier notes? If so, why hadn't they shown up? And why hadn't Emmett Wilder mentioned them? Had Wilder lied to the firm? It was a disturbing thought.

Was it possible Wilder hadn't known about the ongoing tests? Kent searched his memory, trying to remember exactly what Wilder had said when Colin Jamieson had interviewed him. Kent had been present that day, and to the best of his ability to recall the questions and answers, Wilder had said he had been involved in the day-to-day tests and there had been nothing amiss.

Christina had searched the earlier test notebooks. Could she have overlooked something pertaining to the case?

Kent wondered if she was in her office now. She had been avoiding him the past week. And when she hadn't been able to avoid him and they did end up in each other's company, she was totally impersonal—all business. That suited Kent. He would have hated to rehash their differences. He also figured that, given time, Christina would get over most of her anger, and they could work their way into a better relationship. They'd better, because the firm wasn't that big. They were bound to be thrown together many times in the future. He knew he was lucky that for now, while her anger was still fresh, they were working on different aspects of the case, so it hadn't been a problem to keep their distance.

But this discovery of Brasselli's note could be important. He'd better find Christina and ask her if she'd noticed anything else along these lines.

He walked down the hall to Christina's office. The door stood open, but she wasn't there. He walked in, found a yellow pad of self-stick notes on her desk. He scribbled her a note and left it stuck to the back of her chair where she couldn't fail to see it.

As he left her office and walked back down the hall to his own, he ran into Colin Jamieson. "I was looking for you, Kent," Jamieson said, forehead knitted. "I need you to go to Conroe tomorrow and take a deposition from Dr. Yost."

"Okay." Kent mentally juggled his schedule. "What time?"

"He said to be there at two. Call his office and let the receptionist know you're coming."

"Okay," Kent said again. "Uh, listen, there's something I wanted to ask you about. Can you come into my office for a minute?"

Jamieson's frown intensified, and he looked at the expensive watch on his right wrist. "I only have three minutes."

Kent almost smiled, but didn't quite dare. To Kent's way of thinking, the older man was just a little too full of his own self-importance. It hadn't taken Kent long to discover Jamieson also had absolutely no sense of humor. "It won't take long. I just want to show you something I found in going through the R & D notes on the Wilder case."

"What is it?" Jamieson said impatiently, following Kent into his small, crowded office. Kent walked around behind his desk and picked up the notebook he'd been studying earlier. He handed it to Jamieson, opened to page twenty-three.

"Look at the notation on line ten," he said.

Jamieson studied the notation for a long moment, then, with an inscrutable look on his face, he handed the notebook back to Kent. "What about it?" he said, his tone clearly stating that Kent was wasting his valuable time.

"Don't you think it's a little odd that Armand Brasselli should say he was continuing to check a problem, most probably with the steering, when according to Emmett Wilder, there were no problems with the steering?"

Jamieson shrugged, but his dark eyes carried an expression that was not as casual or indifferent as his gesture. "I think you're making too much of nothing," he said. "Forget about it." His voice carried a warning note that Kent would have had to be deaf not to hear.

"But you can't call this notation nothing. Brasselli was referring to something," Kent insisted even as he knew Jamieson would not like being contradicted.

"I do call it nothing," Jamieson said coldly. "The plaintiff's attorneys have already been over these notes, and they didn't question it." He smoothed back the sides of his already impeccably groomed salt-and-pepper hair. "Now, I'm going to be late for my appointment if I don't get going." He turned. "And don't forget to call Dr. Yost's office."

Dismissed, Kent thought. Well, hell, why worry about this if Jamieson thought it was nothing? After all, Jamieson was the senior partner, not Kent. Jamieson had the courtroom experience, not Kent. And Jamieson was calling the shots on this case.

Not Kent.

"Kent's birthday is next Wednesday, and I'd like to give him a birthday party. What do you two think?" Diana asked.

It was the Tuesday after Marcy and Joel's party. Allison, Lee and Diana had just finished dinner and were sitting around the kitchen table.

Lee smiled. "I think that's a great idea."

Allison wasn't sure she agreed, but her reasons were not ones she wanted to try to explain, so she smiled and said, "Me, too. Were you thinking of a surprise party?"

"Well, yes, I was," Diana said. "I thought I'd invite him for dinner. You know. A family celebration. And when he gets here, he'll find all his friends are here, too."

Allison agreed to help Diana plan the party, and for the next week, during which she did not see Kent at all, she kept to her word. Throughout the week, she wondered what Kent was doing. Each night she imagined him and the beautiful Christina together. She tortured herself with images of their kissing the way she and Kent had kissed.

The brightest spot of the week came on the day Diana and Allison were writing out the invitations. Christina's name was not on the list. As if it wasn't important at all, Allison said, "Did you forget about the girl Kent's been dating? You know . . . Christina?"

Diana shrugged. "No, but when I talked to Kent the other day, I very casually brought up Christina's name. It's a good thing I did, because Kent said they're no longer seeing each other."

Allison's heart went *zing* after which she immediately berated herself. Why should it matter to her whether Kent was seeing Christina or not?

But it did matter, and she knew it. She actually began smiling again, and by the day of the party, she was actually looking forward to the evening.

She gave Marianne her bath early that afternoon, and by five o'clock Allison was soaking in a tub full of scented bubbles while the baby lay happily in her crib watching her musical mobile. Allison had left the bathroom door open, and as the music drifted in the air, she remembered the look in Kent's eyes when he'd presented her with the gift for Marianne.

At five-thirty Allison began dressing for the party. Since coming back to Houston, she'd actually gained back about six of the fifteen pounds she'd lost, and she knew she looked better.

At six she was ready to go downstairs. The guests had been told to come at six-thirty. Kent had been invited for seven. Allison took one last look at herself in the full-length mirror. She had chosen to wear a casual summer outfit—black split skirt and a fitted, short black-and-white diamond-print jacket, paired with sheer black stockings and low-heeled black patent leather pumps. With the outfit she wore a clunky silver bracelet and black-and-silver diamond-shaped earrings. She smiled at herself, deciding she was happy with the way she looked.

Diana had insisted on hiring the teenager who lived across the street to sit upstairs with Marianne so that Allison could relax and enjoy herself at the party. After giving instructions to the girl, Allison fluffed her hair one last time, then walked slowly downstairs.

A few of the guests had already arrived, among them Diana's mother, Barbara Kent, and her youngest sister, Jackie.

"Hi, Allison," Jackie said.

Allison smiled at the pretty blonde. She really liked Jackie, who had a perky personality and a nice smile for everyone. She'd had a tough time after her divorce a few years back, but she was doing well now.

"Hello, Allison," said Barbara Kent.

"Hello, Mrs. Kent." After hesitating briefly, Allison walked over and gave Kent's grandmother a hug. Although Allison knew Diana and Barbara were often at loggerheads, she had always liked the cantankerous woman. "It's good to see you again."

For the next fifteen minutes, one guest after another arrived, including Marcy and Joel, Gail and Michael Berry, Nikki and Glenn Prescott and Nikki's mother, Sunny. In fact, most of the people Allison had seen at the Fourth of July barbecue had all been invited to the birthday celebration, with the exception of Christina and Lee's and Diana's co-workers. In their places were some of the people Kent worked with, none of whom Allison knew.

By ten minutes to seven, all the guests had arrived. Lee had made arrangements with several of his neighbors to hide the cars in their various backyards or driveways, so Kent wouldn't be suspicious when he drove up.

Everyone took their places in the living room, and Diana closed the louvered doors that led into the foyer so Kent wouldn't see them when he arrived.

Allison looked around at the thirty-some guests as they all whispered and laughed among themselves. As she did, her gaze met Marcy's, and Marcy grinned at her. Joel, who was standing next to Marcy, his arm around her shoulders, winked.

Precisely at seven o'clock, the doorbell rang. "Shh," said Carol, Diana's sister, and the crowd fell silent. From behind the louvered doors, Allison heard Diana open the door, heard her say "Hi, Kent! Happy birthday," and his cheerful answer.

"Where're Lee and Allison?" Kent asked.

Allison kept her eyes on the closed doors, not trusting herself to meet anyone else's gaze.

"They're having a drink in the living room. Let's go in."

Allison held her breath, knowing everyone else in the room was doing so, too.

Diana opened the doors, and Allison, along with everyone else, shouted, "Surprise!"

Kent's mouth fell open.

Allison's heart felt full as she watched the emotions flicker across his face—first surprise, then delight. He grinned and advanced into the room.

As he greeted people, Allison watched him. He looked even more handsome than usual, she decided, in well-pressed tan slacks, an open-necked burgundy cotton shirt and dark brown loafers.

Eventually he reached her. "Did you have a hand in planning this?" he asked, smiling down at her.

"Yes, I helped, but it was all your mother's idea." She returned his smile. "You really were surprised, weren't you? I was afraid you might guess what she was up to."

"Nope. When she asked me to dinner, I thought, yeah, that would be nice, and never gave it another thought."

"Well, happy birthday."

"Thanks."

They stood there awkwardly, and Allison knew Kent felt just as uncomfortable as she did. There was so much she wanted to say, but she had no right to say any of it. "Where's the baby?" he finally asked. "Sleeping?"

"She may be by now. Diana hired Judy from across the street to watch her tonight."

He nodded, and another awkward moment of silence followed. Then, just as Allison was about to excuse herself to go help Diana in the kitchen, a goodlooking, tall man about Kent's age walked up to them. Allison couldn't remember his name, but she knew he was a co-worker of Kent's.

"Hey, Kent! Great party, huh?" he said.

"Hi, Steve. Yeah, it is." Kent turned to Allison. "Have you two met? Steve Trumbull, Allison Fornier—my stepsister."

"Stepsister, huh?" Steve said, laughing. "Boy, some guys have all the luck!"

Allison smiled, but she wanted nothing more than to escape. She felt too vulnerable right now, too exposed. She wondered if she'd ever be able to handle her feelings for Kent in a way that would allow her to be around him without worrying that everyone else in the room would know exactly what was going on inside her. Finally she made her excuses and walked back to the kitchen, where Diana, along with the caterer she'd hired for the evening, was arranging hot hors d'oeuvres on a large crystal platter.

For the next hour Allison busied herself by tending to the guests. Then, when she felt she'd done all she could to help and really needed to circulate, she spied Marcy and Joel standing off to one corner of the family room that opened onto the kitchen. A few minutes later she joined them.

Marcy hugged her. "So you finally decided to take a break."

"You sure look pretty tonight," Joel said, giving her an admiring glance.

"You'd better watch it," Marcy said. "I'm getting jealous!"

At just that moment, Kent walked up. He smiled at her, then turned to Joel. "Why didn't you tell me about this party?" he asked.

Joel grinned. "I don't tell you everything."

"Oh, yes, you do."

Marcy said, "Hey, he'd better not!"

They all laughed.

"So, what's new at work?" Kent said, turning back to Joel.

As the men began to talk about their respective law firms, Allison chatted with Marcy. But a few minutes later her attention was caught by something Kent was saying.

"And so I decided to ask Colin Jamieson about it."

"Why? Did you think there might be something wrong?" Joel asked.

"Well, not only that, but I was worried about what the plaintiff's attorneys might think. Jesus, this could have blown huge holes in our case!"

"What are you talking about?" Marcy asked.

Allison was glad Marcy had asked the question. Her curiosity was aroused, too.

Joel looked at Kent, and Kent shrugged. He turned to include the two women in the conversation. "I was just telling Joel I'd discovered something that made me think a client of ours might not be telling the truth."

"On the Wilder case?" Allison asked.

His eyes met hers. "Yes."

"So what did Jamieson say when you asked him about it?" Joel asked.

"He said not to worry about it."

"That's all?"

"Yep."

"So are you just going to forget about it?"

"Hell, why not?" Kent said. "I don't get paid to question a senior partner. You know that." Then he laughed. "And I happen to like getting paid. That means I keep my mouth shut."

"But, Kent," Allison said, "if you think something is wrong, you can't just sit by and ignore it, senior partner or not."

He stared at her.

"Well, you can't."

"Why can't I?"

"Because it's wrong, that's why!" She knew this was the wrong time and the wrong place to question his decision, but she couldn't seem to help herself. She didn't like his cynical reply to Joel's question.

"You're the last person I'd imagine who'd feel that way," Kent said.

Allison tried not to feel hurt. He had good reason for thinking this, and she knew it. "And you're the last person I'd imagine who'd let money stand in the way of what's right." As soon as the words were out of her mouth, she knew she shouldn't have said them.

His eyes narrowed. "Can you believe it? Self-righteousness from the original take-the-money-and-run girl."

Stunned by the cruelty of his remark, Allison could only look at him. Suddenly she realized just how much she'd been fooling herself in thinking she and Kent could ever build any kind of relationship again. His stinging indictment of her told her exactly how much anger he still harbored against her. He had never forgiven her, and he never would.

Chapter Ten

Fighting tears, Allison turned and walked away. But not before she heard Marcy say "That was a little cold, don't you think?"

Blindly Allison headed for the powder room. A few seconds later Marcy fell into step beside her. She squeezed Allison's shoulder.

Allison held on to her emotions until they were both in the tiny powder room with the door closed. Then she sat down on the closed toilet seat and buried her face in her hands. She was shaking. "Oh, God, Marce," she said. "He despises me."

"Oh, honey, he doesn't despise you!" Marcy knelt in front of her and gently pulled her hands away from her face. She held them tight. "You know what I think?"

Allison shook her head. She was trying very hard not to cry. Above all, she didn't want anyone else at the party to know she was upset. Knowing how protective her father was, especially now during Marianne's illness, she wanted to avoid a scene where she envisioned his berating Kent. She'd caused enough trouble in this family. She didn't want to be the source of yet another crisis.

"I think Kent is unhappy about the choices he's made," Marcy said, "but he's too stubborn to admit it. Joel has told me about talks they've had, and all is not as wonderful at Keating & Shaw as Kent would have us believe. That's why he lashed out at you. Because you said what we were all thinking. And because Kent feels exactly the same way down deep."

"Do you really think so?" Oh, she wanted to believe Marcy. Marcy was saying what Allison had been thinking, but she'd been afraid, way down deep, that it was wishful thinking. But if Marcy and Joel thought so, too...

"Yes, I really do."

"And you don't think he hates me?"

"No. In fact, I think just the opposite. I think he's still in love with you." Her blue eyes were soft with compassion. "That's why your implied criticism hurt. That's why he struck back. He cares about what you think."

If only Allison could believe Marcy's theory was true.

"Now come on," Marcy urged. "Wash your face. Put on more lipstick. Smile! And let's go out there and knock 'em dead!"

Allison gave her a wobbly smile.

"Good! That's much better."

Allison took a shaky breath. She did feel better.

"Everything's going to be okay," Marcy said as they both stood.

"I hope you're right."

"I am. You'll see."

After Allison walked away and Marcy went running after her, Kent said, "Why is it okay for Allison to say anything she pleases, but when I retaliate, I'm cruel?"

Joel shrugged. "Well..."

Kent put down the empty glass he'd been holding and shoved his hands in his pockets. He looked down at his feet. Although he felt justified in his anger at Allison for criticizing him in front of his friends, he knew he should never have said what he did. Now he felt like a first-class heel.

He sighed. Why had he said what he did? Had he wanted to hurt Allison?

As a lawyer, he knew a case could be made for him. After all, she had hurt his feelings, too. Still, he knew the reason he'd gotten so mad was that she'd only given voice to the doubts that plagued him late at night when he was alone. Doubts he didn't want to acknowledge.

Joel nudged him. "The girls are coming back," he said.

Kent looked over his shoulder. He saw Allison, but she didn't look in his direction. Instead, she turned and walked into the dining room. A moment later Marcy rejoined them. She gave Kent an accusatory look, but she didn't say anything.

"Excuse me," Kent said. "I think I'd better go apologize." He headed toward the dining room. Would Allison forgive him? he wondered.

Just then a new song began to play, piped through the house on the built-in stereo system. When Kent reached the dining room, where the large dining table had been pushed into one corner, he saw that several couples were dancing. Allison stood in the arched doorway leading into the L-shaped living room. Kent threaded his way through the dancers until he reached her side. Walking up behind her, he touched her shoulder. "Allison."

She stiffened.

"I . . . would you dance with me?"

She turned, raising her face to his. Her beautiful golden brown eyes studied him gravely. "Why?"

"Because we have to talk."

She looked at him for another long moment, then, with a small sigh, she said, "All right."

She felt so small and defenseless in his arms. So soft and feminine. And still so fragile. How could he have lashed out at her that way? Especially in light of her personal situation. Why was it that she could always manage to make him forget everything, so that he acted in ways he normally wouldn't?

He pulled her close as they began to dance, and he could feel the shudder that raced through her body. "I'm sorry," he whispered against her fragrant hair. "I had no right to say what I did. You didn't deserve it. Can you forgive me?"

She pulled away a little bit and looked up at him. She nodded. "And—and I'm sorry, too."

His arms tightened around her. "You spoke the truth."

She didn't answer for a minute. "You spoke the truth, too."

Kent wished they were alone. He wished.... But they weren't alone. And wishing wouldn't change the facts. "Are we still friends?"

"Yes."

But as he drew her close again, he knew they were both kidding themselves. It wasn't friendship he was feeling. And he didn't think she was feeling friendship, either.

That night as Allison lay in bed, she remembered every moment of the party. She kept thinking about what Marcy had said. Was Marcy right? Was Kent still in love with her? Was that why he'd been so quick to turn on her when she'd criticized him so thoughtlessly?

Allison knew she wasn't blameless in what had happened. She'd had no right to infer Kent wasn't doing the right thing. No right to judge him. After all, she had certainly made some poor choices in her life.

He'd asked if they were still friends. She'd answered yes. But even as she was agreeing, she knew she wasn't being truthful with him. What she felt for Kent was much more than friendship.

She was in love with him.

She had been in love with him for a long time.

She was afraid she would always be in love with him.

And she didn't know what to do about it.

After a night when he didn't get much sleep, Kent decided he would try to talk to Colin Jamieson one more time. He told himself this decision had nothing to do with what Allison had said to him.

First thing Thursday morning, Kent approached Jamieson's secretary. "Lisa, I'd like to see Mr. Jamieson this morning, if possible."

Lisa looked at Jamieson's appointment book. "You're in luck. He's got a few minutes open around eleven."

"Put me down."

At eleven o'clock Kent headed back to Jamieson's office. After keeping him waiting fifteen minutes, Lisa finally ushered Kent into the large corner office that afforded a spectacular view of Houston's skyline. Sunshine flooded the office, and the sky looked blue as far as the eye could see. Rank definitely had its privileges at Keating & Shaw.

"What is it, Kent?" Jamieson said, looking up from some papers on his desk. He didn't offer Kent a seat.

Invitation or not, Kent sat in one of the two leather chairs positioned in front of Jamieson's desk. He leaned forward. "I've been thinking about that notation I found. You know, the one about the tests on the steering mechanism of the Wild Rider."

Jamieson's eyes hardened.

Refusing to be intimidated by Jamieson's lack of encouragement, Kent plunged ahead. "I'm really bothered by that notation, and I'd like your permission to investigate it further."

"No."

Kent struggled to hold on to his temper. Getting angry wouldn't help his cause, nor would it help his position in the firm. "Sir, I think there's a possibility Wilder is lying to us. Don't we owe it to ourselves to find out the truth? I was planning to interview Brasselli anyway—"

"Now, dammit, Kent," Jamieson said, his face becoming red, "I said 'no.' So don't push it. You're out of line, and I want you to drop the subject. Do you understand?"

"But I—"

Jamieson's eyes narrowed. "I don't want to hear another word about this." His voice carried an implicit warning.

"But, sir, I think—"

"I don't give a damn what you think! And questioning my judgment is not the way to make partner, young man. I hope you realize that."

Kent bit back the sharp retort that threatened to erupt. "Couldn't you at least mention that discrepancy to Ben Keating? See what he says?" Ben Keating was the managing partner of the firm and one of its founders. He was also a good friend of Lee's and had been instrumental in Kent's job offer from the firm.

Through clenched teeth Jamieson said, "This is my case, Sorensen. My case. Not yours. Not Keating's. I make the decisions here. Have you got that?"

"Yes, I—"

"Now," he continued coldly, "do you want to stay on this case or not?"

Kent knew the real question was do you want to stay on with this firm or not? "Yes. I do."

"Fine." Jamieson looked back down at the papers on his desk. "We're finished, and I'm very busy."

"Yes, sir." Kent knew he should apologize, but he simply couldn't bring himself to say the words. He was backing off. That was enough.

Thursday night Marianne took a turn for the worse. In the space of just a few minutes, her color turned dark blue, and Allison, after hooking up the emergency oxygen supply, called Dr. Richardson's beeper number.

Within minutes the doctor called her back. After Allison explained the situation, he said he would send an ambulance. "I'll meet you at the hospital. Don't panic. She'll be all right as long as she's got the oxygen."

White-faced, Allison, Lee and Diana stared mutely at each other as they waited for the ambulance to arrive. All Allison could do as she watched the baby labor to breathe, was pray. *Please, dear God, let it be okay. Let my precious baby be okay. Please don't take her away from me. I know I haven't done much of anything admirable with my life, but please, please, don't punish Marianne. She doesn't deserve it.*

On and on she prayed.

Promising.

Begging.

Bargaining.

She paced and prayed. She looked out of the window and willed the ambulance to go faster.

Finally the ambulance arrived, sirens screaming as it raced down the quiet street. Two paramedics rushed in, and Allison watched as they gently lifted Marianne and carried her downstairs and outside. Within minutes they had her hooked up to the oxygen supply in the ambulance.

"You can ride back here with her, ma'am," said the youngest looking of the paramedics. His freckled face was grave.

"We'll follow you," her father said, giving her a hug then boosting her into the back of the ambulance. Before the door closed, Allison's gaze met Diana's. She saw the fear in Diana's eyes and knew it was a reflection of what her own eyes must show.

The ride to the hospital went by in a blur. Allison held on tight, her eyes never leaving Marianne's little body. She watched Marianne's chest rise and fall, rise and fall, as the same litany of prayer ran through her mind. The siren's wail sliced through the night as the ambulance careered toward its destination.

When they pulled up under the canopied emergency entrance, Allison scrambled out of the vehicle and allowed the paramedics to do their job. Two nurses were ready for them as they entered the brightly lit receiving area. While the nurses took over, Allison answered questions and signed forms.

Within minutes Dr. Richardson joined her. "We're transferring the baby to pediatric ICU," he said. "I'll examine her there."

As the hospital personnel began to wheel Marianne off, Lee and Diana walked through the door. "Thank goodness," Allison said. "I hated to leave here, knowing you were coming, but they're taking her to pediatric ICU."

"Let's go," Lee said, putting his arm around her. Diana took her hand, and they walked together behind the crib on wheels.

Allison was glad for their support. She was afraid that once she was alone, terror would overcome her. This crisis, coming after such a long period where Marianne had done so well, seemed worse because they had been lulled into thinking the baby wasn't as sick as the doctors had originally suggested.

Now Allison knew she was.

And the knowledge terrified her.

Ten minutes later Marianne was settled into an examining room in the unit, and Allison, Lee and Diana were instructed to wait outside in the hallway. "Or you can go out into the waiting area," a kind redheaded nurse said, pointing to the double doors that led outside the section.

"No," Allison said. "We'll wait here." There were no chairs in the hallway, so they stood in a silent, tight little group. Every once in a while, their gazes met, and Allison had to look away. She couldn't stand seeing the fear her father tried to disguise or the compassion in Diana's blue eyes.

As the seconds ticked away, Allison continued her prayers. Her eyes watched the doorway as she imagined what was going on inside the room. They waited and waited for what seemed like hours to Allison.

Finally Dr. Richardson came out of the room. Allison held her breath, fear clogging her throat.

He met her gaze. "That crisis point I warned you of has come, Mrs. Fornier. I wish we could have waited until Marianne was a little older, but we can't."

"Do you mean the open-heart surgery has to be done now?" Allison's voice sounded strange to her, as if it were coming from a great distance.

Diana took her hand again, squeezing it comfortingly.

"Yes," Dr. Richardson said. "We'll make sure she's kept stabilized through the night, and we'll do the surgery first thing in the morning."

Allison bit her bottom lip to still its trembling. *Oh, God. Oh, God. Please, God.*

"Let's go out to the waiting area where we can sit down and I can explain everything to you," the doctor added. "By that time, the release forms should be ready for you."

A nurse wearing the name tag Marilyn Flack explained the various forms to Allison. "Now, about blood," she said.

"Blood?" Allison said.

"Yes. Your daughter will need blood during the surgery. Are you willing to take blood provided from the hospital blood bank, or do you prefer using your own donor?"

Allison looked at her father and Diana. "I don't want a stranger's blood." She turned to the nurse. "I'll give her blood."

"Or I will," Lee said.

The nurse looked at Marianne's chart. "Your daughter is AB-negative, Mrs. Fornier. What's your blood type?"

"A-positive."

"I'm afraid you're not compatible."

"Not compatible! But I'm her mother!"

"That doesn't matter. Was her father AB-negative?"

"I don't know."

"He must have been. I'm afraid the only blood types compatible with your daughter's are AB-negative or O-negative."

Stricken, Allison again looked at her father and stepmother. Lee shook his head. "Like you, I'm A-positive."

"So am I," Diana said.

Allison swallowed. "I—I guess we'll have to use the blood-bank supply." But the thought scared her. She knew labs tested blood thoroughly, but today, with AIDS and its attendant horrors, it frightened her to take even the smallest chance with blood from an unknown source. But what choice did she have? Marianne had to have blood.

Thirty minutes later the papers were signed. "Why don't you go home for the night, Mrs. Fornier?" the doctor asked.

"No! I want to stay here with Marianne," Allison said.

"You're going to need your rest," Dr. Richardson insisted. "Tomorrow is going to be a long day."

Allison shook her head stubbornly. "I'll lay down here, on one of the couches."

Dr. Richardson sighed, meeting her father's gaze. "All right," he finally said. "I'll ask them to give you a pillow and blanket."

"Diana," Lee said, "why don't you go home and get some sleep? I'll stay here with Allison."

"No," Diana said. She smiled at Allison. "If you two are staying, I'm staying, too."

And so the three of them began the long night's vigil. They didn't do much talking. Each was lost in his or her own thoughts.

Lee thought about his little girl and how he wished he could lift this burden from her shoulders.

Diana thought about how much she had grown to love Allison and little Marianne.

And Allison thought about how Marianne was the best part of her and how, if she could, she'd trade places with her.

The clock ticked away the minutes, and they waited.

At seven o'clock Friday morning, Kent's phone rang. "Kent Sorensen," he said as he lifted the receiver.

"Kent? When I tried your condo and there wasn't any answer, I was hoping you'd be at work."

It was his mother.

He tensed. "Mom? What's up?" Diana never called him this early.

"Marianne was rushed to the hospital last night," said his mother's strained voice.

Kent's heart rate shot up alarmingly. "What happened?" He tried unsuccessfully to push his fear down. "Is she all right?"

He heard his mother sigh. "Yes, for now, anyway. She turned so blue, Kent. It was so frightening. It happened so suddenly, about nine o'clock last night. I know

Allison was terrified, but she managed to get the emergency oxygen hooked up to the baby, then she called the doctor. He sent an ambulance, and we all came down here to the hospital. We've been here ever since.''

"But Marianne's okay?"

"Well, no, not okay. Just stabilized. They're going to do the open-heart surgery this morning. She's scheduled to go into the operating room at nine.''

"Oh, man," he said. "Is Allison doing all right?"

"As well as can be expected. She's worried sick, of course. And, well . . .''

"What?"

"Well, last night we found out Allison's blood isn't compatible with Marianne's, and neither is Lee's or mine, so they'll be using blood from the blood bank. Allison's worried about that, and the truth is, so am I.''

So was Kent. "What kind of blood do they need?" Maybe one of his friends could supply blood for her.

"She's AB-negative. Either that or O-negative.''

Kent's heart leaped. "I'm O-negative! Did you forget?"

"I—I guess I did," Diana said slowly.

"I could give blood.''

"Oh, Kent! Would you?"

"What kind of question is that? Of course I will! Notify the nurses or doctors or whatever you have to do. Tell me where to go, and I'll be there in thirty minutes!''

Dr. Richardson allowed Allison to see Marianne for a few minutes before they wheeled her into surgery. The baby had already been given an injection, and she was asleep. Allison's eyes filled with tears as she stared down at Marianne's small body swathed in hospital green and covered by white cotton blankets. An intravenous tube was taped to her tiny hand. She looked so little. So helpless.

Her feathery eyelashes lay against her cheeks, and most of her face was obscured by the nasal prongs covering her nose. Allison bent over and kissed Marianne's forehead, then stood watching as the nurses wheeled her away.

She joined her father and stepmother in the waiting area outside the surgical unit. The large wall clock read 8:57.

"How did she look?" Diana asked.

Allison pressed her lips together. Tears threatened to erupt. All she could do was nod and swallow hard.

"Oh, honey..." Diana said. Both she and Lee got up and put their arms around her.

Allison couldn't control the tears any longer. She didn't want to cry. She'd fought against crying for hours because she was afraid once she started she wouldn't be able to stop. But now her strength seemed to have completely disappeared, and the tears gushed.

Lee gently walked her to the leather couch in the corner and sat her down between them. He kept his arm around her shoulders, and Diana pushed a tissue into her hands.

"I—I'm sorry," Allison said. She swiped at her eyes, then blew her nose. She took a couple of long, shaky breaths. The tears hadn't stopped completely, but at least they weren't coming in torrents any longer.

"Don't apologize," Diana said.

Her father just squeezed her shoulders.

At that moment Allison looked up and saw Kent. A piercing mixture of pain and happiness shot through her as she took in the worry lines furrowing his forehead, the concern flooding his blue eyes and the wonderful fact of his presence.

He walked straight over to her, and she stood. And then, without seeming to care that they were in a public place, that his mother and her father were sitting there watching them, that they were supposedly nothing more than friends, he put his arms around her and tucked her head under his chin.

"Kent," she whispered. "You came."

"Nothing would have kept me away," he said. "I knew you needed me."

And with those words, something hard and tight inside Allison seemed to uncoil and loosen, and she knew that at least some of her prayers had been answered.

Chapter Eleven

"You mean you gave blood?" Allison asked. Kent had just explained about Diana's early-morning call. "Your mother didn't tell me!"

"Well, if anything went wrong, I didn't want to get your hopes up," Diana said. She smiled.

"Oh, Kent. That's wonderful. How can I ever thank you?"

"I don't need any thanks. I care about Marianne, too," he said softly.

Then he took her hand and led her to one of the couches. The four of them settled in to wait. Kent held her hand the whole two hours they waited. At any other time, Allison would have wondered what Diana and Lee were thinking. Right now nothing except Marianne seemed important.

At eleven o'clock, just as Allison was beginning to get really anxious, Dr. Richardson, surgical cap pushed back on his head, walked into the waiting area.

Allison took one look at his weary face set in grave lines, and her heart zoomed into her throat. Kent's hand tightened, and for a moment no one said a word.

Then, as if a silent cue had been given, all four rose to their feet and waited. Allison held her breath, heart pounding.

Then Dr. Richardson smiled, his gaze meeting hers. "Marianne's going to be all right," he said. "The surgery was successful."

Allison's knees nearly buckled beneath her. "Oh, thank God," she said. "Thank God." And then the four of them were all laughing and talking at once.

During the days that followed Marianne's surgery, Allison spent most of her time at the hospital. It was terribly hard on her to see Marianne hurting, because recuperation after open-heart surgery was painful for anyone, and for a baby, who didn't understand what was happening, it was especially difficult. But Marianne, like most babies, bounced back quickly. Within days she was smiling up at Allison, and even though Allison knew the baby's tiny chest still hurt, the pain didn't seem to cloud her sunny disposition.

By Wednesday, five days after the surgery, Marianne was able to take a bottle and she was moved out of pediatric ICU and into a private room in another wing. Allison loved the new room, a colorful red, yellow and green. By the time the flowers and stuffed animals and other gifts that had been sent to the baby were put in the room, it almost looked as if it were Christmas. Marianne seemed to love all the color and stayed awake for longer periods of time.

Allison had a lot of company at the hospital. Diana and Lee came nightly. Sunny and Nikki came. Joel and Marcy came. Michael and Gail Berry came. Her grandparents, who had returned from their safari, came twice.

And Kent came.

Allison knew that she and Kent had reached some kind of turning point the day of Marianne's surgery, and she also knew that once the baby was home again, they would have to talk about their feelings.

Until then she tried to put her emotions concerning him on the back burner. But sometimes, when Marianne was sleeping, Allison would drift into that half state of wakefulness and dreaming where she would conjure an idyllic setting that had no bearing on reality: a two-story white house with a picket fence around it and climbing roses adorning it. Inside the house would be a family—a mother who looked like Allison, a father who looked like Kent and several rosy-cheeked children, the oldest of whom was a little girl who looked the way Allison imagined Marianne would look when she got older.

Only one thing happened to disturb Allison's dreamlike state. One day, while sitting in the lounge at the end of the hall from Marianne's room, Allison was in the middle of one of her romantic fantasies when a young, dark-haired woman walked into the lounge and sat down across from her.

Allison mentally gave herself a shake and smiled at the woman, who gave her a shy smile back. The woman looked familiar to Allison, but she couldn't place her or think where she might have seen her before.

For a while the two of them leafed through magazines, but several times Allison could feel the woman's gaze upon her, and finally she laid her magazine on the coffee table between them and said, "Hi. I'm Allison Fornier, and my daughter is recovering from surgery." She inclined her head toward Marianne's room.

"Hello," said the woman in a soft voice with a slight Spanish accent. "I am Yolanda Gonzales." She smiled, her dark eyes friendly but still shy. "My son, Roberto, is also recuperating from an operation."

They began to talk, and a few minutes later Yolanda said something about Dr. Richardson.

"That's it!" Allison said. "I saw you in Dr. Richardson's office!"

"Oh, yes. I remember," Yolanda said.

That was the beginning of a friendship that built rapidly over the space of the next couple of days. Allison learned that Yolanda was a single mother, struggling to get her teaching degree while working full-time as a secretary. She lived with her grandmother, she explained, who watched Roberto for her. Roberto, who was eight months old, had been born with a hole in the wall between the two upper chambers of his heart—a condition that required surgery to fix. He had had the surgery the day before Marianne had had her surgery, and he was now recovering rapidly.

Allison grew to like and respect the other woman, who had a plucky spirit and had overcome many obstacles in her young life. She couldn't help comparing her own silver-spoon existence with Yolanda's economic struggles.

Gradually, as the two women talked, Yolanda's story unfolded. She had fallen in love with a young man named John Guerrero, who came from a family much higher placed on the social and economic ladder than Yolanda's, and John's parents had disapproved of her. "They thought John was better than me because I have no education and my parents were laboring-class people. They forbid John to see me, and because he worked for his father, he was afraid to defy them openly."

"Oh, that's terrible," Allison said.

"But John and I were seeing each other secretly," Yolanda admitted. "He was trying to figure out a way for us to marry."

"What happened?" Allison asked, caught up in the other woman's drama.

Yolanda's eyes filled with tears. "I—I still cannot believe it myself. John was alone in his father's liquor store when two men came in with a gun. They robbed him, then they shot him. He died on the way to the hospital." Now the tears ran down her cheeks. "I didn't even know about it. He was dying, and I never knew!"

"Oh, Yolanda." Allison's heart constricted with pity. "How awful."

"I waited and waited for him. He was supposed to come to my house after work, and he never came. I—I was afraid to call his house." She wiped at her eyes with a tissue. "I couldn't sleep that night. I kept worrying and wondering. And then, the next morning I heard about it on the news."

"Oh, God," Allison said.

"And do you know what is the worst thing?" Yolanda said.

"No, what?"

"John never knew I was pregnant. He never had the joy of knowing he would be a father."

"Marianne's father never knew about her, either," Allison said softly.

Yolanda sniffed. "Really? Why?"

And so Allison confided in Yolanda, as the other had confided in her. She told her all about Jean Luc and their marriage. She even found herself telling her about Kent.

"Ahh," Yolanda said, dark eyes shining. "Now I understand why he looks at you in a certain way."

Allison could feel herself blushing. Yolanda and Kent had met the previous evening, when he stopped by to see Marianne on his way home from work.

When, on Sunday, nine days after Marianne's surgery, Dr. Richardson released Marianne, Allison hated to call an end to her budding friendship with Yolanda.

She hugged Yolanda and said, "Let's keep in touch."

"I would like that," Yolanda said.

They exchanged addresses and phone numbers. When Lee and Diana arrived to take her and Marianne home, Allison hugged her new friend again. "I'll call you soon," she promised.

Kent decided the San Diego Airport was one of the scariest he'd ever flown into. A white-knuckle flier anyway, he was certain the jet couldn't possibly avoid hitting one of the buildings in downtown San Diego as they made their approach. Miraculously, though, the pilot managed to set the 727 down without a mishap.

This was Kent's first visit to San Diego, and as he drove the rental car up Highway 163 toward Escondido and Poway, he admired the spectacular vistas, so different from the flat terrain of Houston.

He wondered what kind of reception he would get from Armand Brasselli. When Kent's secretary had finally gotten in touch with Brasselli, the former designer had been resistant to talk to Kent. Loretta persisted, though, and finally Brasselli had agreed to see Kent.

Kent had taken the first flight to San Diego. Less than thirty minutes from now, he would meet Brasselli. Fleetingly Kent remembered the closed look on Colin Jamieson's face when Kent had said he wanted to ask Brasselli about the terse notation concerning the "continuing" tests on the steering mechanism—if that's what the note had meant. Kent had not been able to uncover a single other reference to any ongoing tests—to the steering mechanism or any other part of the Wild Rider. And when he'd finally talked to Christina about the subject, she said she'd seen nothing at all in the notebooks she'd studied.

Kent knew Jamieson would not be happy if he found out about Kent's trip to San Diego. Routine questioning of Brasselli could have been handled via a phone call. And routine questioning was all Kent had been authorized to do.

But Kent wanted to see Armand Brasselli's face when Kent introduced the subject of the notation. In fact, Kent had copied that page of the notebook and brought the copy along with him so that if Brasselli for some reason denied knowledge of it, Kent could produce the proof that the notation had actually been made.

Kent exited Highway 163 at the Poway exit and turned right, following the twisting four-lane road around the mountain and into Poway proper. Without any difficulty, he found the condominium complex where Brasselli and his wife lived. As Kent pulled into the entrance to the hillside community of pink stucco units garlanded with deep-red-and-purple bougainvillea, Kent mentally prepared himself for the impending interview.

Brasselli answered the door himself. He was a stocky, dark, good-looking man who appeared to be in his late fifties. He was dressed in shorts, sneakers and a T-shirt. The T-shirt stretched over some impressive muscles. "You Sorensen?" he demanded. He didn't smile.

"Yes." Kent did smile and extended his hand.

Expression warming slightly, Brasselli took his hand and they shook. Brasselli's grip was powerful. Kent wondered if the man lifted weights and vowed he would get back to some serious exercising himself. Soon.

Brasselli ushered Kent into a sunny, multiwindowed living room furnished in a comfortable, southwestern decor. Kent liked the look of the place with its russet-colored tile floor and open spaces. He sat on the sand-colored sofa in response to Brasselli's gesture and absentmindedly petted the head of a friendly yellow Lab who had materialized at his side.

"Would you like a drink?" Brasselli asked. "Beer? Scotch? Iced tea?" He looked at the dog. "Benjamin, don't make a pest of yourself!"

"How about a glass of water?" Kent said. He smiled down at the dog. "He's not a pest."

The Lab wagged his tail. When Brasselli returned to the living room with Kent's glass of water, he gave the dog a curt order, and the Lab walked a few feet away and settled down in a patch of sunlight.

A few minutes later Kent pulled out his small tape recorder.

Brasselli's eyes narrowed. "What are you doing that for?"

"I'm going to record our interview," Kent said matter-of-factly. He pulled his notes from his briefcase.

"Why?"

"Because I don't take shorthand, and I don't want to make any mistakes when I transcribe my notes later."

Brasselli thought about that for a minute, then said, "I told your secretary I don't know anything useful."

"Let me be the judge of that," Kent said. "Sometimes witnesses think they don't know anything when they actually do. Besides, you will definitely be called as a witness by the plaintiff. We need to know what to expect."

"Well, let's get this over with. I'm supposed to play golf at three o'clock."

Kent looked at his watch. It was just after one. "No problem." He met Brasselli's gaze. "Ready?" When Brasselli nodded, Kent turned on the tape recorder and spoke into the mike, giving the date, time and case reference. "Now, Mr. Brasselli, were you involved in the initial design of the Wild Rider?"

"Yes." Brasselli settled back in his chair.

"Can you tell me what your position was?"

Brasselli began to detail his involvement and responsibilities as the head of the design team.

Kent continued with routine questions about the progression of the design. After twenty minutes of questions and answers, Kent said, "In going over the R & D notebooks on the testing of the Wild Rider, I came across a notation you made last November." Casually he opened his briefcase and extracted the copy of the page containing the note. The note itself had been highlighted in yellow. "Take a look at this please, and translate the notation for me."

Brasselli, face impassive, accepted the paper. He studied it silently. The room was very quiet—the only sounds were those of the traffic on the highway below and the occasional thump of the dog's tail as he eyed them from his vantage point nearby.

Kent waited.

Finally Brasselli looked up. He shrugged. "It's nothing important."

"Even so, would you translate it, please?"

Something flickered in the depths of Brasselli's dark eyes. "I'm not sure I remember what this note meant."

"Try."

"Okay." Brasselli looked down at the paper again. "I'll try. Uh...continuing to check Wild Rider..."

Kent nodded. He'd figured out that much himself.

"...for problem with..."

Kent held his breath.

Brasselli looked up again. "Strength."

"Strength?" Kent didn't even try to hide his skepticism. "What does that mean?"

"You know, fork strength."

Kent met the man's gaze steadily. "You're sure?"

"Positive." Brasselli's dark eyes never even flickered.

"Because," Kent said slowly, "if this note didn't refer to fork strength and instead was related to *steering*, we'd have a serious problem, wouldn't we?" The word steering hung in the air between them.

"Well, it doesn't," Brasselli said, his answer clipped and final sounding.

"Would it surprise you, Mr. Brasselli, to learn that the crux of the suit being brought against Wilder's involves a faulty steering mechanism? *Knowledge* of a faulty steering mechanism?"

"Oh yeah?"

Brasselli's pretense of ignorance didn't fool Kent. He knew the man had known. He also suspected Brasselli was lying about the notation. He only wished he could prove it. "Yes."

"Did you have any more questions?" Brasselli asked. He very casually laid the copy of the notation on the table beside him.

"No, I don't think so." Kent turned off the tape recorder. "Thank you for seeing me." He returned his notes to his briefcase. "I'd like that copy back, please."

Brasselli said, "Oh, yeah, sorry."

Kent could have sworn his innocence was feigned.

But on the flight back to Houston, as Kent thought about the interview with Brasselli, he wondered if he'd imagined Brasselli's culpability. Maybe Kent was so hung up on the idea that Emmett Wilder was lying he had read something more into Brasselli's answers and expressions than had actually been there.

And even if Kent was right and Brasselli and Wilder were both lying, if he couldn't prove it, what difference did it make?

Kent returned to the office on Thursday. He'd only been gone one day. At eight-thirty Thursday morning, his intercom buzzed and Loretta said, "Mr. Jamieson wants to see you in his office."

"Now?" Kent had an appointment in fifteen minutes.

"He said right now."

Had Jamieson somehow learned about the interview with Brasselli? Kent wondered as he walked to Jamieson's office.

"I thought I told you to drop the matter of that note," Jamieson said without preamble as Kent entered his office.

Kent girded himself for what he knew was coming. "Yes, you did."

"Then why the hell didn't you?"

"I don't know what you mean."

"You know damn well what I mean!" Jamieson said. "You went out to San Diego and interviewed Armand Brasselli and asked him about that notation. Now, don't try to deny it, because Brasselli himself told me."

Brasselli himself told him! If ever Kent had needed proof that there was something fishy with this case, Jamieson's disclosure clinched it.

"I'm warning you, Sorensen," Jamieson said. "And this is your last warning. Forget about this. Because if you don't, if I hear one more thing that you've done or said to stir this up again, you're history around here." He yanked a folder from the top of his In box and opened it. He began to read.

What the hell was going on? Kent decided then and there that he would not try to make any excuses. "I had always intended to interview Brasselli in person. I'm sorry if you think I should have told you ahead of time. I never imagined you'd object to being thoroughly prepared for trial. Brasselli will damned sure be called as a witness by the plaintiff. I was only doing my job. *Sir,*" he added.

Jamieson did not answer. In fact, he didn't look up.

Kent walked out of the office, ignoring the secretary's wide-eyed stare. Obviously she'd heard everything Jamieson and Kent had said. Kent grimaced. Knowing Lisa, by noon everyone in the firm would know about the confrontation.

Sure enough, later that morning Christina, giving him a smug look, said, "You'd better watch your step, Kent. I have a feeling your days here may be numbered."

Kent gave her a hard stare. Enough was enough, and Christina was beginning to get on his nerves.

For the rest of the day, while working on other things, Kent kept thinking about Armand Brasselli and Colin Jamieson's reaction to a perfectly legitimate interview and the cryptic notation itself. Was he being unreasonable about this? Was Jamieson right? Should he just forget all about it?

Finally, after going around and around and coming up with no answer that satisfied him, he decided he would stop by his mother's house after work and talk to Lee. He respected Lee's judgment and his integrity, and he'd be interested in hearing what the older man thought.

He'd intended to be on his way no later than seven o'clock, but it was nearly eight before he actually left. Then he decided to make a quick stop at his condo and change clothes. Thirty minutes later he'd changed into jeans and a dark blue cotton shirt and was heading out the door again. By the time his car was cruising up Memorial Drive toward the Loop, the sun had disappeared in the west, and dusk had settled over the city.

He had not seen Allison since she'd brought Marianne home on Sunday. He had purposely avoided going to the house because he knew Allison, as well as he, needed some time alone. They had spent several emotional hours together at the hospital—hours where they'd made a quantum leap in their relationship—and he wanted to give her time to think about it before he saw her again. But now he was going to see her.

He wondered how she'd act. Would she be happy to see him? He wondered what she'd think if he told her what he was preparing to tell Lee. At least she couldn't accuse him of sitting by and doing nothing, the way she had the night of his birthday party.

By the time he reached the house and pulled into the driveway, the night sky no longer carried any traces of the setting sun. Indigo shadows fell across the hood of the Corvette as Kent climbed out of the car and walked to the gate. It was locked, so he pushed the buzzer mounted into the brick wall, and a few moments later the speaker box crackled into life.

"Yes?"

It was Allison's voice. Kent said, "Allison, it's me, Kent."

"Oh—oh, just a minute." A second later he heard the click, which meant she'd released the lock on the gate. He opened it and walked through, closing it carefully behind him. By the time he got to the front door, she'd opened it. Light spilled out onto the walkway, and Allison, partially hidden from his view, stood behind the opened door. He walked inside, then turned to face her.

His breath caught, and for a moment he wasn't sure he'd ever breathe again. All he could do was stare at her. He wouldn't have been surprised to find that his eyes had bugged out of his head.

She was dressed for bed. Clinging to her curves was a pale peach satin peignoir trimmed in peach lace, covering, Kent was sure, a matching nightgown. The shimmery material fell sensuously over her hips and legs to just skim the floor. Peeping from beneath the hemline were bare feet with pink polished toenails.

As Kent's gaze traveled the length of her body and back up, he could see a pulse beating in the hollow of her throat, and he could also see the outline of her nipples clearly defined under the revealing fabric. His heart began to beat faster, and he couldn't tear his eyes away from her.

When he finally looked up and their gazes met, he could see she was as disconcerted as he was. Her cheeks were flushed, and she stammered a little when she said, "I . . . uh . . . I didn't expect anyone, so I . . ." Her voice trailed off, and she hurriedly shut the door and crossed her arms protectively across her breasts.

Kent found his voice and was surprised that it sounded normal. "I'm sorry. I should have called, I guess. I came to see Lee."

"He's not . . . they're not here."

"Oh. When will they be back?"

Allison's flush deepened. "Th-they're gone until Sunday night. They went to New Orleans."

"New Orleans! I just talked to Mom yesterday morning, and she never mentioned it."

"I know. My dad had unexpected business there, and on the spur of the moment, Diana decided to go with him. Then they thought they might as well stay the weekend, too." She was clutching the sides of the peignoir as if afraid it would suddenly fall open, and Kent knew she was mortally embarrassed by her state of undress.

"Damn. I really wanted to talk to your father." They were still standing, facing each other in the foyer, and Allison didn't seem to have any inclination to move. Suddenly unsure of what his next move should be, Kent wavered between saying he guessed he'd be going and walking into the living room and sitting down.

"Listen, Kent, I . . . uh . . . you're welcome to stay and visit awhile, but I think I'll just go upstairs and put on something else." She started toward the stairs.

"No, Allison, wait. It's okay. You don't have to do that. I'm only going to stay a minute. In fact, if you want me to, I'll leave now." God, she looked beautiful. He couldn't bear for her to take off the peignoir set. He could look at her dressed like that every moment for the rest of his life.

"Well..." She hesitated, indecision clouding her lovely eyes. She sighed. "Okay. Come on in the living room. I just poured myself a glass of wine. Do you want some?"

He smiled. "Sounds good." He'd prefer beer but decided not to push his luck. He followed Allison into the living room and tried not to notice how the sleek material of her peignoir molded to her sweet little bottom. His pulse had gone haywire, and his jeans felt uncomfortably tight. To cover up his growing agitation, he said, "How's Marianne doing?"

"Oh, she's doing wonderfully!" Allison answered happily. "She's asleep. I put her down about thirty minutes ago."

Allison walked to the bar at the end of the room and uncorked a bottle of wine. She began to pour him a glass.

Kent looked around. He could see that she had been sitting at one end of the white sofa because her wineglass and the baby monitor were nearby and an open magazine lay on the cushions. He sat at the other end of the sofa and concentrated on getting his emotions and his raging hormones under control.

She walked back, handed him the glass of wine and sat on the other end of the sofa. She carefully pulled her peignoir closed, but if she were trying to look more modest, it was a losing battle.

Kent thought he had never seen her look more desirable or feminine. Her cheeks still had that flushed color that told him she was embarrassed to be caught half dressed. Her hair, worn in its usual casual style, curled damply around her face as if it had been freshly washed. She wore no makeup; there was only a hint of color on her full lips. As he watched, she caught her lower lip between her teeth and chewed on it—something he knew was a nervous habit.

Finally she looked at him. "Why did you want to see Dad?"

Kent hesitated, then told her everything, including his doubts about the truthfulness of the things he'd been told—both by Colin Jamieson and Armand Brasselli, as well by Emmett Wilder. "Anyway, Jamieson told me to drop the whole thing." He hesitated. "I'm thinking of going to Ben Keating, though. Telling him everything."

"You should, Kent. You can't just drop it. Not now. You know there's something wrong."

"It's not going to do me or Shelley Petrowski a hell of a lot of good if I get fired," he said reflectively.

"You won't get fired. Your instincts are right. I know they are. Go to Ben Keating. Tell him what you suspect. I'm sure he'll back you up."

"Keating might tell me exactly what Jamieson told me."

"Kent..." Allison's eyes looked like liquid gold as she faced him. "Do you really want to work for a firm that practices that kind of law? Can you live with yourself if Wilder really did know there was a design flaw and let Greg Petrowski test the motorcycle anyway? It sounds to me as if there's a cover-up going on."

Kent nodded. She was saying exactly what he'd been thinking. "You're right."

She smiled then, a blazingly beautiful smile, and something tightened in Kent's chest as their gazes met and held. Kent suddenly became aware of how quiet it was and, even though the room they were sitting in was enormous, of how very intimate it felt lit only by the soft light of two lamps.

He stood, and without thinking or planning, he suddenly found himself standing over Allison and reaching for her hand. Without hesitating, she placed her hand in his and allowed him to pull her up and into his arms.

She raised her face. She was breathing fast, and he knew she was feeling all the same chaotic emotions he was feeling. He looked into her eyes, silently asking a question, and read the answer in the depths of her golden brown irises.

He bent his head, and his lips met hers—at first gently, then with more intensity. He wrapped his arms around her, feeling her softness meet his hardness. His heart thundered in his ears, and his blood pounded through his veins as Allison's mouth opened under his.

He drove his tongue deep into the heated recesses of her mouth, and he could feel her body trembling as she responded. He could hear her heart racing, could feel the soft swell of her breasts against his chest and the firm flesh of her back and small, rounded bottom as his hands roamed up and down her body, pulling her ever closer.

He wanted to brand her, to possess her, to make her irrevocably his.

He tore his mouth from hers, dropped his lips to the sweet hollow of her throat. He inhaled her scent, tasted her silky skin with the tip of his tongue. "Allison, oh, Allison. I want you."

She stiffened, and Kent went rigid. Suddenly all the times in the past rose up to haunt him. All the times they'd kissed and touched. All the times she'd pulled away just as Kent reached the peak of his passion. Just when he wanted her the most.

She was pulling away again.

He'd been fooling himself. She hadn't changed. She would never change. Once more she was going to send him home in the night, aching and miserable.

And then, so softly he almost thought he'd misunderstood her, she whispered, "Oh, Kent. I want you, too."

He stared down into her eyes—those beautiful eyes that had looked so sad for so long. "Are you sure?" he asked, his voice sounding rough to his ears.

She smiled, and the brightness of joy shimmered in her eyes, pushing away the last traces of sadness and sending a corresponding joy shooting through Kent.

"I've never been more sure of anything in my life."

Chapter Twelve

Allison thought her heart was going to burst as Kent kissed her. Suddenly her entire world went out of control, as if instead of spinning on its axis, it had tumbled out of the groove and was careening wildly through space. She was a chaotic mass of feelings—a euphoric mix that stunned her with its intensity. And when he touched her, all her long-buried needs erupted.

Then he said he wanted her, and for one long moment her needs were stilled as she absorbed the importance of his words. Now was the time to pull back if she had any doubts at all. Now was the time to call a halt if she wasn't sure. As his hands gripped her shoulders, she could feel the stillness in him. She knew her answer, the next few seconds, would determine the course of the rest of her life. Would Kent be forever relegated to the past? Or was he going to be part of her future?

Suddenly all the regrets, all the mistakes, all the sadness receded, leaving only a certainty that she belonged with Kent.

She always had.

And she always would.

And so she told him she wanted him, too. And her heart was filled with a blinding joy, a brilliant light that pushed out the darkness and sorrow and regrets of the past. When Kent swooped her up into his arms and began to climb the steps, Allison knew she was finally doing something right.

Kent carried her into her bedroom and set her down, but he still kept his arms around her, as if he were afraid if he let her go she might change her mind. She reached up and held his face with one hand on either side. They looked at each other for a long moment, then he bent his head and kissed her. This kiss wasn't as greedy as the one he'd given her downstairs. This kiss said he knew more would come so he could afford to take his time. This kiss promised and enticed, and when it was over, Allison was shaking with need and the force of her turbulent emotions.

Smiling down at her, Kent began to unbutton his shirt. Still a little shy about the mechanics of lovemaking, Allison wasn't quite sure what to do. Tentatively she reached over to help him, and she heard his quick intake of breath as her fingers grazed his chest.

More boldly she pulled his shirt open and slowly ran her palms over his warm skin, feeling the strength and power under the steady rise and fall of his chest. His chest was smooth, with only a few whorls of hair down the middle. Allison leaned forward and kissed him. She could feel his heartbeat under her lips as he gathered her closer.

He buried his face in her hair, whispering, "Allison. I've dreamed of this for so long."

She lifted her face to gaze into his eyes, which looked as dark as the midnight sea in the dimly lit room. "I know. I have, too."

They kissed again, and then she helped him remove the rest of his clothes until he was clad only in his briefs. She wanted him to take those off, too, but she still felt too shy around him to say so. Still, she couldn't resist touching the waistband, and that was all the hint it took. Kent hurriedly removed the briefs and then straightened.

Allison's breathing accelerated. He was so magnificent. So splendid. So completely male. She was awestruck by the beauty of his body. Why had she never realized just how beautiful a man's body could be? she wondered.

And then he was undressing her. Untying the sash of the peignoir and allowing the wispy material to slide off her shoulders and fall in a shimmery pool at her feet. Allison shivered as his fingertips grazed her collarbone then slowly trailed down to touch her breasts. She arched into his touch. He continued to caress her, touching her first with gentle fingertips that whispered erotically over her satin nightgown, and then bending to continue worshiping her body, but this time with his lips and mouth. The barrier of the nightgown intensified Allison's arousal, and she trembled under the onslaught of feelings.

Finally, just as she thought her knees would no longer support her, Kent reached down and lifted the nightgown over her shoulders, and the last barrier between them was gone.

Later, after he'd led her to the bed and they were lying next to each other, he began to touch her again, stroking her body and kissing her mouth at the same time. And Allison, who wasn't sure how much of this sweet torment she could stand, began her own exploration of him.

"Yes, yes," he said as she closed her palm around him, feeling his heat and strength, trembling in anticipation of the moment she'd dreamed about and thought would never come. She loved the feelings he was awakening in her, feelings that she never knew would be so powerful. She loved the way he touched her, each intimate stroke an affirmation of his need for her and hers for him. It was so good to finally allow herself to let go and just feel, to think of nothing except this man and this moment.

She never closed her eyes. She wanted to see him as he made love to her. She wanted to know what he was feeling. She had waited so long for this, and she wanted to experience every second to the fullest. She loved it when he moaned as she touched him. She loved it when she felt him tremble. And she loved it when his hands were no longer so gentle but became demanding and insistent.

She smiled when Kent said, "I can't wait any longer." She opened to him, welcoming his thrust, reveling in the feeling of completeness and unity as he pushed farther, settling deep inside her.

They began to move together, finding the rhythm that was theirs, fitting their bodies together in a timeless dance of love.

He thrust.

She received.

He inserted.

She surrounded.

He pushed.

She lifted.

Their moves were intricate yet simple. Primitive yet delicate. Ageless yet wondrously new.

Allison felt as if she were on a Ferris wheel, inching her way to the top as her heart pounded faster and her breath became more labored and her body tensed in expectation of the free-fall to come.

And then she reached the top, and for one breathless moment she trembled there at the edge of the world. Kent, too, seemed to still, then with one mighty thrust, he spun her off into the universe with him.

She wanted to cry.

She wanted to laugh.

She wanted to shout.

She wanted this feeling to go on forever. As his life force spilled into her, she kept her legs tightly wrapped around him, and she looked deeply into his eyes. "I love you, Kent," she whispered. "I've always loved you."

The look on his face caused her heart to squeeze painfully. And then he kissed her. And kept kissing her. Her mouth. Her eyes. Her nose. Her throat. And over and over he said, "I love you. I love you. I love you."

Much later, after tiptoeing down the hall and peeking in at Marianne, who was still sleeping soundly, they made love again—slowly and sweetly—savoring each moment while whispering words of love to each other.

And afterward, as they held each other, they talked. "Did you love Jean Luc?" Kent asked, and Allison knew he needed to know.

"No. At first he excited me and made me feel special. But I never loved him. And I think he knew that. I think that's why..." She broke off. She didn't want to talk about her marriage tonight. Not tonight.

Kent's arms tightened around her. "We don't have to talk about it now."

She understood that eventually they would have to. And that was okay. As long as it wasn't tonight.

Still later she said, "When I found out you'd gone to work for Keating & Shaw, I felt as if someone had kicked me in the stomach."

His body tensed against hers. "But why? Isn't that what you wanted me to do?"

"Yes, but after I married Jean Luc, after everything in my life fell completely apart, the one thing that kept me going was knowing I'd done the right thing by releasing you from our engagement. It made me happy to know that at least *you* were happy. That you were following your dream. And then, to find out you weren't... I felt betrayed." There. She'd said it. Now she tensed, waiting for his answer.

It was a long time in coming. Finally in a low, thoughtful voice he said, "Somehow nothing worked out the way I thought it would. Without you my dream seemed hollow." He laughed without mirth. "You've heard that old saying, haven't you? The one that goes 'be careful what you wish for...'"

"'...because you may get it,'" Allison finished softly.

"I think that's what happened to us." He kissed her ear, his warm breath sending a pleasurable tingle down her spine. "I think we both got what we thought we wanted, and it turned out to be different from what we'd imagined."

"We were both too young."

"And too self-centered."

"No, I was the one who was self-centered," Allison said.

"I have to take my share of the blame, too," Kent insisted. "I refused to see that you were just being practical. That we needed more than love to live on."

"But we would have managed! I know we would have. I should have trusted you."

"Things would have still turned out the same. I still had some hard lessons to learn."

Allison decided he was being gallant in trying to accept blame, and she should allow him that gesture. She loved that about him. That he wanted to make her feel good about herself. Well, finally maybe she would be able to feel good about herself. Because now it looked as if she would be given a second chance.

With his fingertip he traced the line of her chin, then brushed his fingers over her lips. "Allison, do you think we've grown up enough to make a success of our relationship this time?"

The question trembled in the air. Allison held her breath, and in the muted light she met Kent's gaze. His eyes glowed, and her heart began to beat in slow thuds as the importance of his words permeated her body.

"Can we try again?"

"Try again?" she said, afraid to let her hopes go as far as they wanted to.

"Yes. Try again." He smiled down at her. "I want you to marry me. Will you?"

Allison blinked back tears as she whispered fiercely, "Oh, Kent! Yes, yes. I'll marry you!"

His kiss was like a benediction and a promise, and as Allison wound her arms around him and held him close, she vowed she'd never let anything come between them again.

* * *

Early Friday morning Kent went home, showered, shaved and dressed for work. Then he packed an overnight bag and tossed it into his car. He would spend the weekend with Allison. They would wait together for Lee and Diana to return and tell them about their engagement.

He hummed all the way to work. Even the prospective talk with Ben Keating—a talk he'd promised Allison he'd initiate first thing this morning—couldn't dampen his glowing happiness.

He hadn't felt this good in years. Memories of the previous night tumbled through his mind, and as he entered the office, he was smiling.

"My, don't you look happy this morning," said Barbara, the receptionist.

Kent headed straight for Ben Keating's office.

"I'm sorry, Kent, Mr. Keating is on vacation."

Even this news couldn't dampen Kent's spirits for long. "For how long?"

"He'll be back Wednesday."

As Kent headed for his office, he decided he could wait until Wednesday. And then, because nothing could keep his thoughts away from Allison for long, he began to count the seconds until he'd see her again.

Things were meant to turn out this way, he thought. If he and Allison had married years ago, neither would have been ready. They had both matured. Both learned lessons. Kent knew he was much better equipped to care for her and Marianne than he would have been before—both financially and emotionally.

And care for them he would. Allison and Marianne were now the two most important things in his life, and he would do anything he had to to safeguard their future.

* * *

Allison couldn't wait until Kent came back on Friday night. All day long, as she fed and bathed and played with Marianne, she thought about Kent and their lovemaking.

Poor Jean Luc, she thought. She had never ever felt about him the way she felt about Kent. Jean Luc's lovemaking had never moved her the way Kent's did. Everything between her and Jean Luc had been superficial—all flash, no substance. No wonder their marriage had been a disaster.

Except for Marianne. She smiled as she cuddled the baby. She guessed everything had worked out the way it had been meant to work out. If she and Kent had married four years ago, not only would she not have had Marianne, but she and Kent wouldn't have been ready to build the kind of life she knew they could have.

All day long she dreamed rosy dreams about how she would help Kent regain what she had cost him. How together they could make something wonderful out of the mistakes of the past. How, working side by side, they would build a future based on all the values Kent had once held dear. Values she was certain he still held dear.

And eventually they would have a child—a little sister or brother for Marianne to grow up with.

Allison touched her stomach. Maybe even now she was pregnant with Kent's child. Oh, that would be wonderful!

Finally six o'clock came. Allison was ready, trembling, eager. While Marianne had napped that afternoon, Allison had gotten everything ready, feeling wicked even as her heart fluttered with excitement and anticipation.

And then Kent was there, his eyes bright, his smile warm. The moment he closed the door behind him, he pulled her into his arms and kissed her greedily. "I missed you," he said, kissing her again and again. "Let's go make love," he whispered into her ear.

"We can't yet. The baby's awake."

He laughed and looked around. "Where is that little cutie?"

Allison's heart expanded. She could hear the genuine love in his voice. She gestured toward the living room. "In there. Sitting, waiting in her little chair."

While Kent played with Marianne, Allison watched him. Every once in a while his eyes would meet hers, and they'd share a warm, intimate look. He was good with the baby. She liked him and responded to him. He would be a wonderful father.

Later, while Marianne, who had already been fed, lay nearby in her stroller, Allison and Kent ate their dinner. Allison had fixed baked chicken and rice and served it with salad and rolls. They laughed and talked and Kent told her about having to wait until Wednesday to talk to Ben Keating. They drank some wine, and after dinner he helped her clear off the table and load the dishwasher.

Then together they got Marianne ready for bed. Kent sat and watched while Allison rocked the baby to sleep. Then quietly they carried her upstairs and placed her in her crib. Allison switched on the baby monitor, then turned to Kent.

He smiled, reaching for her hand. "Is it my turn now?" he murmured as they walked out of the room together.

She smiled and nodded.

He put his arm around her and turned her toward her bedroom.

"No," she said. "I have something else in mind." She felt like a kid on Christmas day. She couldn't wait to see his face when he saw what she'd done. Taking his hand, she led him into the master bedroom suite. When he frowned, she said, "Don't worry. Come on."

He followed her into the adjoining master bath. Ever since Allison had first seen this bathroom, she'd wanted one like it. The bathroom was enormous—almost as large as a bedroom—and in the center of it was a huge sunken tub. Overhead was a large skylight, which was now glowing orange from the evening sun.

As Kent, eyes questioning, watched, Allison turned on the taps. Smiling, she poured scented oil into the steaming water. Then she picked up the book of matches sitting on the vanity and began to light the candles in the dozen or so crystal holders placed around the room. She looked at him over her shoulder. "What are you waiting for?" she said.

Kent thought he'd died and gone to heaven when Allison, eyes bright with excitement, joined him in the tub. She lowered herself into the water and leaned back against him. The hot water and scented oil and flickering candles, combined with the feel of her against him, caused Kent's heart to try to explode out of his chest. His hands trembled as he stroked her slippery skin.

She laid her head back, and he closed his eyes. She felt better than anything he'd ever experienced before. The fact that he loved her, and she loved him, that she'd planned this, all added to his pleasure.

He cupped her high, firm breasts, feeling the hard nubs grow even harder as he teased them, and his own body quivered in response. "You feel so good," he whispered in her ear.

"I love when you touch me," she said.

They stayed in the tub a long time. They kept draining the cooled water and adding more. They touched and kissed and brought each other to the peak of pleasure more than once.

And then later they went to Allison's bedroom, where they slept in each other's arms.

On Saturday they took Marianne outside and settled her in her chair, shaded by an umbrella, and they lay in the sun and swam in the pool and cooked hot dogs on the grill.

Saturday night they sent out for Chinese food. Kent helped Allison bathe Marianne and put her to bed. Then, of course, they went to bed themselves.

Sunday morning they had a long, leisurely breakfast, after which they cleaned up the house together, played with the baby and settled in to wait for Lee and Diana to come home.

"They said they'd be home about three," Allison said.

"Before they come, there's something I want to give you," Kent said. He smiled at her, then reached into his pocket.

Allison frowned a little when she saw the jeweler's box. He could almost hear her thought processes, the questions running through her mind: When did he have time to buy a ring? Why didn't he ask me to come with him?

He watched her face as she opened the box. He knew the instant she realized the ring was the one he'd given her during their first engagement. He could see her hands were shaking as she lifted the ring from its satin bed.

"Oh, Kent," she said. She raised her face, and her eyes were bright with tears. "You kept it. All this time, you kept it."

"Let me put it on you."

When Kent saw the ring sparkling once more on Allison's hand, his chest expanded with pride. That ring belonged there. This time it would remain there.

Then he kissed her because his heart was too full to speak and because he wanted to.

Afterward she smiled up at him. "No wonder I love you," she said, her voice not quite steady. "You're incredibly sweet to me."

"It's easy to be sweet to you." He smoothed a strand of hair back from her face and thought about how much he loved her. Tears still shimmered in her eyes.

"What if I'd never come home? This ring is worth a lot of money. You should have taken it back."

"Aren't you glad I didn't?"

And then they kissed again. Finally Allison said, "We'd better stop. My father and your mother will be here soon."

Lee and Diana arrived home about twenty minutes after three. They came in the back door, and Kent and Allison, along with Marianne in her jumper chair, were sitting in the kitchen waiting for them.

"Hi, Kent," Lee said, setting down the two suitcases in his hands. "We saw your car out back."

Kent stood. Allison remained seated, hiding her hands in her lap. She didn't want her father or stepmother to see the ring until after they'd told them about their engagement.

"Have you been here long?" Diana asked, walking into the room.

"Did you have a good time?" Allison interjected. She knew Kent would not want to answer his mother's question. At least not right now.

"We had a wonderful time," Diana said, but her eyes were bright with curiosity as she looked first at Allison and then back to Kent.

"New Orleans is a great place," Lee said. "The only problem is, we ate too much." But his expression was quizzical, too.

"What's going on?" Diana asked. "You two look very pleased about something."

Kent looked at Allison. She put her hands on the table. The diamond was impossible to miss.

Diana's mouth fell open. Lee's face broke into a huge grin. Kent started to laugh and walked around to where Allison was sitting. She stood, and he put his arm around her.

"We're getting married," he said.

Allison knew her father was happy for them, but she wasn't sure how Diana felt. She watched her stepmother's face carefully. And then Diana smiled, and Allison felt weak with relief.

Just then Marianne cried out, and they all turned to look at her. She laughed and stuck her fist in her mouth. And then they were all hugging and talking at once.

"This is the way things were always meant to be," Lee said, hugging Allison.

Marianne cooed as if to say she agreed with that sentiment, and Allison was sure that this time nothing could happen to mar her happiness.

Chapter Thirteen

Allison floated through the next couple of days on a rosy pink cloud. Even the fact that it was difficult for her and Kent to be alone couldn't affect her happiness for very long.

It was especially difficult for them to make love. And now that they'd finally consummated their love, it was really hard not to be able to express it whenever they wanted to.

But they managed.

Allison smiled, hugging herself. The previous night—Tuesday—Diana and Lee had offered to watch Marianne, and Kent fixed dinner for Allison at his place. They'd hardly eaten any of the dinner. They'd tried, but they couldn't keep their hands off each other. Finally, laughing a bit guiltily, they'd abandoned their steaks and given in to the powerful emotions raging through them.

Allison squirmed as she remembered how they hadn't even made it to Kent's bedroom. Instead, they'd hurriedly undressed each other and made love right there on the dining-room floor.

She'd loved it.

And that in itself amazed Allison. She'd always thought of herself as rather prudish. Oh, she'd been wildly attracted to Kent during their first engagement, and she'd wanted to make love with him, but she'd never imagined that she could be so abandoned. So—so *wicked*. She'd never been that way with Jean Luc. And Jean Luc had been a skillful and knowledgeable lover. But somehow, when Jean Luc made love to her, she'd always known exactly what was happening, as if she were an observer and not a participant. Her mind would think, now he's touching me there and I'm supposed to feel thus and so. And she would. But she had always been in control of her emotions. Never once had she slipped over the edge. Never once had she given herself completely.

Allison daydreamed away most of Wednesday morning thinking about making love with Kent. She had finally realized that the reason she would never let Kent make love to her during their first engagement was that deep down she was never certain of his commitment to her. She had never been sure he would be able to make the choices necessary for them to have a good life together. If only she'd been able to see that the choices Kent made were the right choices.

She frowned. If only she didn't feel so responsible for Kent's defection from the storefront practice. For the cynicism and disillusion he felt.

It was so ironic that she finally understood what Kent had tried to tell her, and he no longer seemed to care.

Well, all that would change now. Allison was sure that now that they were back together, Kent would regain some of his idealism and eventually would even want to go back to the storefront—at least on a part-time basis.

Actually it might be very nice if Kent could stay at Keating & Shaw, as well. Her father had once explained to her that it would be much easier for Kent to accomplish the kinds of things he wanted to accomplish with the storefront once he'd built a name for himself with a firm like Keating & Shaw. A big firm had all kinds of resources behind it and could actually enhance Kent's work with the storefront. Kent would have the prestige and exposure of high-profile clients and still do the important work of the storefront.

We could have our cake and eat it, too!

Thinking about this, Allison looked at her watch. It was almost noon. She wondered if Kent had been able to talk to Ben Keating yet. She mentally crossed her fingers. Hopefully the talk would go well. She couldn't wait to find out what Ben Keating had had to say.

At eight o'clock Wednesday morning, Kent had called Ginny, Ben Keating's secretary. She'd informed him that, yes, Mr. Keating was back in the office, but he was extremely busy and couldn't possibly see Kent today.

"I only need five minutes," he said.

"He doesn't have five minutes." Her voice had taken on that don't-you-understand-how-important-he-is tone that always amused Kent. For some reason, most of the secretaries in the firm were competing in some kind of unacknowledged game of my-boss-is-more-important-than-your-boss, and they never missed a chance to reinforce their superiority.

"Look, Ginny, this is important. Don't play games with me, okay? Let me talk to him." Now that he'd decided to talk to Ben Keating, he didn't plan to wait another day.

He could hear the rustle of paper, and he imagined her looking at the great man's calendar as she pondered whether she should grant this favor to the lowly serf. A few minutes later she came back on the line. "If you're here exactly at ten minutes to twelve, I'll see that he works you in for a couple of minutes before his luncheon engagement." This was said in a tone of great condescension.

"I'll be there." Now he could afford to be nice. "And thanks, Ginny. I really appreciate this."

At ten minutes to twelve, Kent stood outside Ben Keating's closed office door. Two minutes later the door opened, and Keating beckoned to him.

"Kent," he said. "Come on in." He smiled.

Kent smiled back. He liked Ben Keating. Had liked him from the very first time he'd met him.

Kent followed Keating into the sunny office with its view of southwest Houston. Keating, a tall, distinguished-looking, gray-haired man with sharp, dark eyes, seated himself behind a beautiful old carved mahogany desk. "So what can I do for you, Kent?" he asked. He gestured toward the whiskey-colored leather chairs grouped to one side of his desk.

Kent sat and crossed his legs. "Well, sir, something's come up on the Wilder case that disturbs me."

"Oh?"

Kent explained what he had discovered when reading through the R & D notes. "It appears to me that the design team knew there were structural problems with the steering. If I think so, it's a sure bet the plaintiff's lawyers will think so. And once they get their hands on that, our case is down the tubes."

"Did you talk to Colin about this?"

"Yes, sir. And he brushed me off. You know we've got to produce all those documents within two weeks, and if we don't have a better explanation for that note than Brasselli gave me, or at least something to show they resolved the problem—whether it was with the fork strength or the steering mechanism, as I suspect—those sharks will eat Brasselli for lunch in his deposition. Not to mention what they'll do to us in front of the jury."

After he'd finished, Keating pursed his lips and studied Kent for a few minutes. "Listen, son, Jamieson is one of the sharpest and most respected trial lawyers in the state. If he doesn't think there's anything to worry about, I'm afraid I have to respect his many years of trial experience and bow to his superior judgment." He paused. "And so do you."

"I understand that, but—"

"Furthermore," Keating said, his voice a little sterner than it had been, "you've already been told all of this. By Colin Jamieson, who is, after all, the attorney in charge of this case. Now, I'll overlook your breach of etiquette in coming to me because you're young and you're relatively inexperienced, but I don't want it to happen again. From now on anything you have to say can be said to Colin."

Kent knew better than to persist. Ben Keating had made himself clear. A wise employee knew when to retreat. Kent thanked Keating for his time and went back to his own office.

All afternoon he fumed. He was caught between a rock and a hard place. Frustrated and angry, he reviewed his options. He could forget about that damned notation and get on with his assignment, which was what he'd been ordered to do.

Ordered! That still rankled.

Or he could ask to be removed from the case. If he wanted to keep his job, he'd drop this hot potato. Because if he asked to be removed from the Wilder case, he might as well resign from the firm, for he would be signing his own death warrant. He would have no future with Keating & Shaw.

Kent didn't call until nearly five o'clock.

"Did you talk to Ben Keating?" Allison asked.

"Yes."

"What did he say?"

"I don't want to talk about it over the phone. I'll tell you tonight." His voice softened. "It's okay if I come over tonight, isn't it?"

Allison laughed happily. "Of course. Do you want to have dinner with us? My father's making stuffed flank steak. He told me to invite you."

After they hung up, Allison wondered about Kent's reticence when she'd asked about his conversation with Ben Keating. Maybe things had not gone well.

Later that evening, after they'd had dinner with Lee and Diana and put Marianne to bed, they walked outside and sat on the deck where they could talk privately. They didn't turn on the outdoor lights or the pool lights, and the darkness wrapped itself around them. Off in the distance heat lightning streaked the sky, and Allison wondered idly whether it might rain later. "So tell me about Ben Keating," she said.

"Well, he said essentially the same things Colin Jamieson said."

"What do you mean?"

She heard Kent's sigh. "I mean he told me to back off. He told me I was completely out of line in coming to him."

"Oh, Kent!" Allison couldn't believe it. She had been so sure Ben Keating would see that Kent was right about this and Colin Jamieson was wrong. "What are you going to do now?"

He didn't answer for a moment. Then softly he asked, "What do you think I should do?"

She wanted to tell him what she thought. But something, some odd reluctance she couldn't identify, told her not to. "Kent, I can't make your decision for you. I tried that once, remember?"

"Will you support my decision, no matter what it is?"

Allison's heart skipped a beat as she realized what he was asking her. As she realized for the first time that maybe the old Kent really was gone forever. "Yes," she answered. She could live with whatever he decided. She loved him and he loved her. That was what was important. But down deep she knew there was no reason to worry. Kent couldn't have changed so much. He would make the right decision.

Wouldn't he?

On the Saturday night after their engagement, Allison received a call from Yolanda Gonzales, her friend from the hospital. She'd already talked to Yolanda several times since Marianne's release, and she was worried about Yolanda. She seemed depressed, even though—like Marianne—Roberto had made a rapid recovery from his surgery. Allison, wanting to cheer up her new friend, invited Yolanda and Roberto to come along on a picnic she and Kent had planned for Sunday afternoon.

Sunday turned out to be a very hot day, but Allison figured it would still be nice in Memorial Park. Marianne, who looked better and better every day, cooperated by taking a long nap early in the day and waking up an hour before Kent arrived.

By three o'clock they were on their way.

"How do you like this car I rented?" Kent asked. "I'm thinking of buying one like it."

"But what about your Corvette? I know how you love it."

"A Vette isn't exactly a family car, and now that I'm going to have a family. . ." He smiled and reached over to touch her hand.

"But we could get a family car for me to use, and you could still keep your Corvette," Allison insisted. "I was planning to buy a car, anyway." She and Kent had not discussed money yet, and Allison wondered how he would feel about the fact that she had an awful lot of it. She'd had a trust fund, set up by her Marlowe grandparents, before marrying Jean Luc. But now, because Jean Luc had been heavily insured, she was wealthy.

"We'll see," he said. "We don't have to decide anything this minute."

Thinking about the money, Allison felt a bit uneasy. Kent had a lot of pride. He might not want to use any money he considered Jean Luc's. Never one to borrow trouble, Allison put the uncomfortable thought out of her mind. She'd cross that bridge when she came to it.

She glanced at Kent. She wondered what he was thinking about. She wondered if he'd come to any decision about the firm and his future there. She wanted to ask him, but she still felt that strange reluctance she'd felt the other day. Surely it wouldn't be long before he came to the same conclusion she'd reached.

But what if he doesn't? What then?

Firmly, telling herself everything would be all right, she put that thought away, too.

It didn't take long to get to the park. Even though it was a blistering hot day, there were hundreds of people there. Even the jogging trail that followed the curves of Memorial Drive was full.

"Look at all those people running in this heat. Are they crazy?" Kent said as they pulled onto the main road leading into the park. "It must be one hundred degrees right now."

"They're gluttons for punishment, I guess." Allison had never been able to figure out the allure of running, even when the weather was nice. But now? In the worst heat of the afternoon? She'd take a nice aerobics class in an air-conditioned room any day. And if she was going to be outdoors, an early morning tennis game or a brisk swim in cool water was much more sensible, not to mention tolerable.

"Where's Yolanda meeting us?" Kent asked.

"By the tennis courts." Allison hoped they would be able to find Yolanda easily. She needn't have worried. Yolanda, with Roberto in a little portable stroller, was waiting exactly where she said she'd be.

Fifteen minutes later the five of them were settled on a quilt under the shade of an enormous ash tree. Roberto, eyes wide as he watched everything, sat in his stroller, and Marianne gurgled happily in her jumper chair.

Allison leaned back, thinking how much she would have hated doing something like this a few years ago. A picnic in the park would not have held any appeal at all. But now, with her new maturity and Marianne's birth, everything seemed entirely different to her. Her gaze drifted to Kent, who, arms propped on his knees, watched as a couple of little boys cavorted with their dog, a friendly golden retriever. They kept throwing a stick, and the dog would bound off, retrieve it and bring it back, tail wagging.

Kent fit this atmosphere perfectly, she decided, envisioning many more Sunday afternoons spent in just this way.

She looked around. The park was filled with people having fun, laughing and talking, eating and playing. Somewhere close by, someone was playing the radio. The station had to be an oldies station, Allison thought, because all the tunes seemed to be vintage rock and roll. The catchy music added to her sense of happiness and well-being.

Now her gaze wandered to Yolanda and stopped. Some of Allison's pleasure faded as she realized Yolanda didn't seem very happy. There were worry lines in her forehead, and her dark eyes were clouded as she stared off into space.

"Is something wrong, Yolanda?" she asked.

Yolanda looked around. "No, no, it's nothing," she said. She darted a glance at Kent.

Kent, after exchanging a look with Allison, said, "You can talk in front of me."

Allison smiled at him. He was such a kind man. Jean Luc had not been kind.

"John's mother has found out about Roberto," Yolanda said, her gaze meeting Allison's. "She has contacted me."

"Is that so bad?" Allison asked. She turned to Kent. "The John she's referring to is Roberto's father. He died before Roberto was born."

Kent's gaze flicked to Marianne, and Allison knew he was thinking, just like her father. She nodded sadly. She wondered if that's why she had been drawn to Yolanda from the start. Because their situations, so dissimilar in some ways, were so similar in this one important part of their lives.

"John's parents hated Yolanda," Allison continued, wanting Kent to understand her friend's fear. "They thought he and Yolanda were no longer seeing each other, so when he died, they had no idea Yolanda was pregnant."

Kent nodded. "Well, is it so bad that they know about Roberto now?"

"Yes!" Yolanda said. "You don't know them, Kent. They are ruthless people. And John was their only child. If I thought they would just want to be part of Roberto's life, that would be one thing. After all, I am not without sympathy for them. I lost John, too, so I understand their grief." Her eyes took a bleak look, and Allison's heart contracted with pity. "But they wouldn't be content to just share Roberto. They would want to own him, just like they tried to own John. I am very frightened."

"Kent, what do you think she should do?" Allison asked.

He shrugged. "There's nothing to do. It would be different if they'd made some kind of move, but they haven't." He looked at Yolanda. "Have they? Have they said anything?"

She frowned. "No. They've just said they want to see him."

"Well, then you have to make a decision."

"I don't want them anywhere near Roberto," Yolanda said fiercely. She put a protective hand on Roberto's head, and in response, he stuck his fist in his mouth and sucked noisily.

"Tell them that, then."

"But what if they insist? Can they force me to let them see him?"

Kent shrugged. "If they can prove Roberto is their grandchild. Can they?"

Yolanda nodded miserably. "I—I put John's name down as the father on the birth certificate."

"Oh, Yolanda!" Allison said, although she understood Yolanda's reasons. She had loved John. She had never dreamed his parents would see the birth certificate.

"I know," Yolanda said. "I was stupid. I didn't want them to know about the baby, but I never thought...." She gazed off into the distance, shoulders drooping, misery stamped all over her.

Allison reached over to take Yolanda's hand. "Don't worry, Yolanda," she said softly. "It'll be okay. They can't force you to do anything you don't want to do."

Yolanda looked up. "I'm afraid of them. They have so much money. They have such good lawyers. John used to tell me about their lawyers."

Allison looked at Kent. An idea formed. "Kent," she said slowly. "You could call John's parents for Yolanda. You could tell them how she feels. Maybe if you called—you know, the voice of authority—they'll back off.''

Kent shook his head. ''I don't think—''

''Oh, please, Kent, would you?'' Yolanda pleaded. Hope shone from her eyes.

Kent shot a look at Allison. A look that told her he was not pleased with her offer of his help. Sighing, he said, ''All right. I'll call them for you.''

Allison smiled. ''Thank you, Kent,'' she said.

''Yes, Kent. Thank you,'' Yolanda echoed. ''And God bless you.''

Later, remembering the conversation, Allison decided it was fate that Yolanda had needed Kent's help. Perhaps by helping her, Kent would finally see where he belonged. Perhaps Yolanda's plight would remind him of all the thousands of other people who felt helpless in the face of insurmountable problems and inadequate resources.

Yes. That's exactly what would happen. Then he would once more be the Kent he used to be. The Kent she wanted him to be again.

Chapter Fourteen

Kent wished he'd never agreed to call John Guerrero's parents. But it had seemed so important to Allison that he help Yolanda, and he had wanted to please Allison. He thought Yolanda was making a mistake, though. He understood her fear of the Guerreros, but life would be so much easier for her if she would just call them and try to work out something that would make them happy.

He had tried to tell her this, but she had been adamant. So he'd agreed to call them for her.

He placed the call at ten Monday morning, deciding he might as well do it now and get it over with. A soft-voiced woman answered the phone, saying, "Guerrero residence."

"I'd like to speak with Mrs. Guerrero, please." Kent had decided that he would talk with Ann Guerrero instead of her husband, because she had initiated the contact with Yolanda.

"Who is calling, please?" asked the soft-voiced woman.

"Kent Sorensen. I'm an attorney calling on behalf of Yolanda Gonzales."

"One moment, please."

He heard a muffled conversation in the background and deduced that the woman who'd answered the phone had placed her hand over the receiver while she told Ann Guerrero who he was. A few seconds later a firm, no-nonsense voice said, "This is Ann Guerrero. What can I do for you, Mr. Sorensen?"

"I'm calling at the request of Yolanda Gonzales, Mrs. Guerrero."

"Why couldn't she call me herself?" Now Guerrero sounded belligerent.

Kent kept his voice neutral. "I'm sorry, Mrs. Guerrero, but Miss Gonzales prefers to have no direct contact with you."

"I see. And what about my request to see my grandson?"

Kent had promised Yolanda he would try to bluff Guerrero, even though he was sure the bluff wouldn't work. "She's considered your request to see her son, but she's decided to deny it."

"Does Miss Gonzales really think that I will just roll over and go away? Conveniently forget about my grandson?" Her voice was tightly controlled, but Kent could hear the underlying fury. "If that's what she thinks, she's sadly mistaken, Mr. Sorensen. My husband and I have no intention of going away. We have a right to see our son's only child, whether Miss Gonzales likes it or not!"

"I'm sorry, Mrs. Guerrero. I know this is not what you wanted to hear. However, Miss Gonzales is Roberto's mother. And she's made her decision." Kent purposely did not refer to Roberto as Mrs. Guerrero's grandson. One of the first things a lawyer was taught was to never reveal anything you weren't required to reveal.

For the first time since Ann Guerrero took his call, some of her control slipped. "Well, you can tell that—that . . . woman . . . that she has not heard the last from us!"

After they'd hung up, Kent called Yolanda at work and relayed the conversation to her. "I don't think she's going to drop this, Yolanda," he warned. "She sounded like the kind of woman who would call her lawyer today and instruct him to take you to court and try to get a judge to grant her visitation rights."

"But Roberto is *my* son. Can she do that?"

Kent heard the panic in Yolanda's voice. He felt sorry for her, but there was no sense in giving her a false sense of security. "It's been done before." Successfully, too, he thought.

"And what happened in those cases?"

"According to Texas family law, if the Guerreros can prove it's in the best interest of the child for them to have a part in his life, the court can rule in their favor."

"Oh, no! Kent, what will I do? They have money and connections."

"Well, don't panic yet. There's no reason to do anything until they make a move. You should just be prepared. I'll talk to a friend of mine whose firm does a lot of *pro bono* work of this type. His name is Joel Bartlett, and I think you'll like him. I'm sure he'd be happy to represent you if you need a lawyer."

"I don't want anyone else," she said, desperation edging her voice. "I want you."

"Yolanda, I'm sorry. I work for Keating & Shaw, and frankly I know you can't afford our rates. Joel is a good friend of mine, and he'll do a good job for you." He hesitated, then decided he'd give her his best advice. "Look, Yolanda, I know how you feel about the Guerreros, but why don't you talk to them? Wouldn't it be better for everyone concerned if you could work out something with them? Wouldn't it be better for Roberto? Is it really fair to deny him a relationship with his grandparents?"

"No. No. Because I know what would happen. They would gradually take Roberto away from me, just as they tried to take John away from me. They don't approve of me, Kent. They think they're better than I am. And even if they didn't take Roberto, they would try to turn him against me. I don't want him to have anything to do with them."

Kent sighed. He was afraid that in the end the Guerreros would prevail, anyway, no matter what Yolanda wanted. As she had said, they had both money and clout. Yolanda had neither. On top of that, she was just managing to eke out a living for herself and her son. And he knew she had a fairly large medical bill to pay. A judge might think he was doing her a favor if he allowed the Guerrero grandparents to be a part of Roberto's life, especially if they offered financial help.

Well, he'd done what he could to help and advise her. Allison would be happy.

Allison wasn't happy. She stared at Kent as he repeated his conversations with Ann Guerrero and Yolanda. "But, Kent! Why couldn't you represent Yolanda?"

"I told you. I couldn't take her case outside of the firm. And she can't afford our prices."

"But surely Keating & Shaw do some *pro bono* work, too. All the big law firms do!"

"Yes, a small portion of our business is devoted to *pro bono* work, but I'm not currently assigned to that section. In fact, I'm not slated to serve in that capacity until sometime next year."

"But couldn't you talk to—"

"Allison, look, it's not just that." He ran his hands through his hair in a gesture of frustration. "I don't want to get involved in this."

"But why not?" She couldn't believe what she was hearing. Why, the old Kent would have jumped to Yolanda's defense. The old Kent loved representing the underdog. The old Kent would have been chomping at the bit.

"Because I no longer take on lost causes."

"Lost causes? You mean you think this would be a hopeless case?"

"Yes. I think she'll lose if the Guerreros decide to press the issue. After all, they *are* Roberto's grandparents, and they have a right to be a part of his life." He took a swallow of the drink she'd prepared for him, then added, "And as long as we're being truthful, I might add that I agree with that."

"You agree with that! Kent! You know what Yolanda told us. You know how those people tried to break her and John up. You know what they're like. They're ruthless and cruel."

"Allison, everyone makes mistakes. Maybe they were doing what they thought was best for their son. Don't you have any sympathy for them? Their only child is dead, and all they have left of him is Roberto.''

''You're making them sound like saints.''

''No. They're not saints. I know that. But they are human beings. I just think, for everyone's sake, Yolanda should first try talking to them.''

''If she should decide to follow your advice, would you represent her then?''

He sighed wearily. ''No. But I'm sure Joel will.''

''I—I don't understand.'' She'd been so sure Yolanda's plight would set Kent back on the track he'd forsaken. ''I thought you'd want to help her. In the old days—''

''This isn't the old days.'' His voice hardened. ''I have a different kind of job now. Different priorities.''

''I—I can't believe you really feel this way.''

''Well, believe it, because I do. Hell, I'd have thought you'd be happy about the fact that I want to provide you and Marianne with a secure future.''

''But, Kent—''

''Damn it, Allison, nothing you say is going to change my mind about this. Now can we just drop it?''

Stung by his answer, she said, ''I suppose the next thing you're going to tell me is that you've decided to stay on the Wilder case.''

He set his drink down on the redwood table next to him. He stared at her. ''I haven't decided about the Wilder case yet. But I thought we'd agreed that whether I stayed with it or not, you'd support me.''

''But I never thought—''

''Oh, I see,'' he said coldly, his eyes narrowing. ''You never thought I wouldn't see things your way, did you?''

''That's not fair, Kent! I just meant—''

"I know exactly what you meant. You thought I'd come around to your way of thinking. You always think I'll come around to your way of thinking. You know, Allison, you tried to manipulate me once before. It didn't work then, and it's not going to work now!"

With a sinking heart, Allison realized Kent still harbored bitterness toward her. Despite his love for her—and she didn't doubt that he loved her—he hadn't completely forgiven her.

Still, she couldn't give up. She couldn't pretend she was happy about the way he'd changed. Furthermore, she didn't believe he really had changed. All this cynicism, all this indifference, was just a barrier he'd thrown up to avoid being hurt again. Eventually, when he trusted her enough, when he trusted *life* enough, the old Kent would emerge. All she had to do was be patient.

But after Kent left to go home, doubts began to creep into Allison's mind. And late that night, right before she finally fell asleep, she admitted to herself that she was afraid.

At nine-thirty the following morning, Kent wearily rubbed his forehead. He felt frustrated and irritated after arguing with Allison over Yolanda's situation and his own situation here at Keating & Shaw.

He guessed he wouldn't have been so sharp with her if he hadn't been feeling so many doubts himself. He wished he knew what to do about the Wilder case.

The Wilder case.

Over and over he'd thought about that damned notation. He didn't know why it kept cropping up in his thoughts. No one else at the firm seemed to think it was a problem. Armand Brasselli said it had to do with the fork strength of the bike and had nothing to do with the steering. Nowhere else in all the dozens of test notebooks was there any mention at all of a problem with the steering. So why was he still doubting?

While his mind was thus occupied, there was a sharp knock on his door. Then it opened, and his secretary walked in, closing the door behind her. "Mr. Sorensen, Jackson Clemente and Tracy Higgins are here."

Kent frowned. "Already? They weren't scheduled to come until tomorrow." Clemente and Higgins were with the law firm representing Shelley Petrowski. The motion for production of documents on the Wilder case had been filed the previous week, and Clemente and Higgins had made arrangements to examine the documents the following day.

"Well, I guess somebody got their signals crossed, because they're here now," Loretta said.

"Oh, hell. And Jamieson's in Galveston today." Great. Now when they discovered the notation that Brasselli had made, Kent would be the one who would have to try to downplay its significance. Who would have to pretend it wasn't a hole in the defense.

"Yes, Jamieson's gone. That's why Lisa sent them to you," Loretta said.

"Okay. I'll get them set up. Have you notified Christina?"

"Yes," Loretta said. "She's on her way. Where do you want them to go? The conference room?"

"Yes. And Loretta? Call Lisa and ask her to come to the conference room, too. If Clemente or Higgins want copies of any documents, I want her to make them. That way she can assure Jamieson that everything was done according to hoyle."

Although it was Keating & Shaw's responsibility to allow the plaintiff's attorneys access to all documentation pertaining to the case—as well as to allow them to copy anything they wanted to copy—they also had a right to oversee the entire process. In other words, Keating & Shaw had the right to protect themselves and their evidence from either destruction or disappearance.

Ten minutes later Jackson Clemente and Tracy Higgins were busily examining the first of the documents, all of which had already been assigned their Bates numbers—an identification numbering system set up by the court. This system made each document easily identifiable and simplified the presentation of the evidence introduced during the trial.

Lisa, Jamieson's secretary, sat at one end of the conference table, and Christina sat at the other. Kent wondered if it were really necessary for him to be there, too. He walked down to Christina's end and said sotto voce, "Are you planning to stay here the whole time?"

"Yes. Why?" Her gray eyes studied him coolly.

He knew she was still nursing a grudge over his treatment of her, but he guessed she was entitled. He made his voice pleasant. "Well, it's just that I have some things to do. I thought, if you're agreeable, I could take care of some of my work while you're in here, and this afternoon you can do something else, and I'll take over here."

She leaned back in her chair and said, "I'll stay the entire time."

"That's not necessary. We can split it up."

"Maybe I don't want to split it up. Maybe I think the Wilder case is the most important thing I have to do."

Then, with a sly smile she said, "Colin asked me to be present."

Colin? Since when had she graduated to a first name basis with Jamieson? Continuing to keep his voice low, he said, "If you want to take charge of this, fine. But if anything happens—" he gave her a meaningful look "—call me immediately!"

Her smile turned smug. "Don't be such a worry-wart, Kent," she murmured, casting a glance in the direction of the two lawyers, who weren't paying any attention to them as they organized their work. "Believe me, everything is under control." Her eyes glittered as her gaze met his.

After Kent returned to his office, he kept remembering the smug look on her face when she'd said everything was under control. How could everything be under control when that damned notation existed? And why had she used that particular phrase? He knew it was probably just coincidence that she'd used that particular choice of words, but he couldn't shake the feeling that there was something not quite right about Christina's remark.

He told himself he was reading something into her remark that wasn't there. He told himself she was just needling him because she knew he'd had some misgivings over that notation, and she liked the fact that Jamieson and Keating had not agreed with him. He told himself she liked pretending she was in the know and he wasn't.

Still . . . he couldn't shake his apprehension, if that's what it was.

For the remainder of the morning, Kent deliberately put his misgivings out of his mind and dictated a batch of letters and a deposition. When he finished, it was nearly noon. Christina hadn't called him once.

He decided, despite her assurances, he would check on things in the conference room. Maybe Christina had changed her mind about staying with Clemente and Higgins the entire day and would want to be relieved for lunch. If so, he would ask Loretta to get him a sandwich, and he would eat in the conference room.

When he got to the conference room, Jackson Clemente had just pushed his chair back. He stood. "I think Tracy and I will grab a bite to eat before we continue," he said, looking first at Kent, then at Christina. "Either of you two want to join us?"

"Thanks, but I've got plans already," Christina said, standing, too.

Kent was relieved. The last thing he wanted was to spend his lunch hour in Christina's company. "Sounds good," he said to Clemente.

They decided to go to Treebeard's, which was one of Kent's favorite lunch spots, even though the food was heavier than he knew was sensible for lunch. The only other problems with Treebeard's were the noise level and the crowds of people who always packed the place to the rafters.

Once the three of them had gotten through the cafeteria-style serving line and were settled at their table with plates of red beans and rice—Treebeard's specialty—Clemente, a short, swarthy man with intelligent, dark eyes, buttered a piece of corn bread and said, "So, counselor, how's the defense coming along?"

Kent laughed. "Nice try, counselor. The defense is coming along just fine."

Tracy Higgins, a young associate about Kent's age, grinned. "That's what they all say," she quipped. Kent liked Tracy. When he'd been working out of his storefront, he'd run into her several times in court. She was bright and personable. Just the kind of lawyer he'd have liked to work with.

Clemente chewed his bread, then said with a wink, "We're gonna win this one, you know. You won't even get to the fifty-yard line." He smiled. "So what are you gonna do about that?"

Kent rolled his eyes. Clemente was an ex-football player who peppered everything he said with football terminology. "As my father would say, when in doubt, punt."

Tracy laughed again and poked Clemente with her elbow. "Notice how Kent's learned all the lawyer tricks?"

"Lawyer tricks?" Kent said.

"Yeah, you know. Never answer a question directly."

"I thought our motto was Always Answer A Question With Another Question," Kent countered.

"That, too," she said.

They made small talk throughout the rest of lunch. But as they were walking back to the office, Clemente said, "You know, Kent, I was really surprised to hear you'd gone to work for Keating & Shaw."

"Oh? Why?"

Clemente shrugged. "Well, you were really making a name for yourself when you had your storefront. And you never seemed like the Keating & Shaw type."

"What type is that?" Kent hated the stiffness he heard in his voice, but he was getting mighty sick of people acting as if he'd committed a felony by leaving the storefront.

"Oh, hell, you know. Razor-cut hair, expensive suits, power ties, sports cars, the right address..."

Kent forced a casual-sounding chuckle, because Clemente's remarks were a little too close for comfort. "I suppose you're going to pretend to be above all that." He gave Clemente's Italian loafers, expensive European suit and diamond tie pin a pointed look.

Clemente grinned. "I never said I was perfect."

Tracy said, "Oh, quit giving Kent a hard time. Let's get a move on. We've got a lot of work to do this afternoon."

But Kent couldn't get Clemente's words out of his mind. Did everyone think he'd made a mistake going to work for Keating & Shaw? He knew his mother had been disappointed, of course, but she'd never said anything. That was one of the things he liked best about his mother—her belief that people should make their own decisions and lead their own lives. She had always supported him, no matter what he did.

He frowned. That was what he wanted in a wife, too. That was what he wanted, *needed*, from Allison. And that was what Allison had said she would do. But would she? If push came to shove, would she?

Allison spent the day looking at houses. She left Marianne with her great-grandmother Marlowe, and Sunny Garcia took her around to see the houses she'd lined up.

"Kent said the two of you had decided on the West University area," Sunny said as they started out from Diana's office on upper Memorial Drive.

"Yes," Allison said doubtfully. Kent liked West U. Well, she did, too, but she thought the area was too expensive, especially since she knew Kent didn't want to use any of her money. But Joel and Marcy lived in West U., and Kent seemed set on it, so Allison had reluctantly agreed.

After looking at half a dozen houses, Allison fell in love with the seventh—a refurbished Colonial on a wooded lot. It was more money than Allison thought they should spend, but she had to admit that the house was perfect for them. It had four bedrooms and two full bathrooms upstairs, and a living room, dining room, kitchen, half bath and a small room that could be used as a study downstairs.

All the original moldings had been refinished, and the floors were the original hardwood. Allison especially loved the *porte cochère* and the glassed-in sun porch that extended across the back of the house.

As she and Sunny walked through the upstairs, Allison could just picture Marianne in one of the two smaller bedrooms that faced the back of the lot, which was south. The room would be sunny and bright the entire day, just right for a little girl. And the other bedroom would make a perfect playroom.

She sighed. If only Kent would allow her to use some of her money, they'd have no problem buying the house, no matter what he ultimately did. Still . . . what difference did it make, really? Even if he was adamant about doing this on his own now, when he finally came to his senses regarding the firm, if they were already committed to buying this house, he'd have no choice but to use her money.

Allison smiled to herself. "Sunny," she said, "I think I'll call Kent this afternoon and tell him about this house. Can you make an appointment for both of us to come back here tonight?"

* * *

Christina was already seated in the conference room when Kent, Clemente and Tracy Higgins walked in. For some reason, even though Kent told himself not to let her get to him, her insistence on staying there during the afternoon needled him. But two could play her little game, he decided.

"I'm going to get some coffee. Would anyone else like some?" he asked.

Christina eyed him from her vantage point at the end of the long table. "Thank you, I'd love some."

"Coffee would be nice," Clemente said.

"And I wouldn't mind a diet soda," Tracy said.

Lisa, who was also back from lunch, stood. "I'll help you, Mr. Sorensen."

When they returned with everyone's drinks, Kent sat across the table from the two rival lawyers. He pulled his appointment book out of his briefcase and pretended to study it. Out of the corner of his eye, he saw Christina staring at him. He wondered if she would get up and leave. She didn't.

Throughout the afternoon he watched and waited. When Tracy picked up the first of the R & D notebooks, he slid a glance Christina's way. She wasn't looking at him.

At three-thirty both Clemente and Tracy were deep into the R & D notebooks. Clemente closed one with a slap and handed it to Lisa. "I've marked the pages I'd like copies of," he said.

Lisa took the notebook and headed toward the copy center.

Clemente picked up the next notebook in line. Kent saw the cover dates and knew it was the notebook containing Brasselli's notation. Without alerting Clemente to the fact that this particular notebook interested him,

Kent kept a surreptitious eye on the other lawyer as he slowly read his way through the pages.

Kent counted the pages silently. When Clemente turned from page twenty-one to page twenty-two, Kent held his breath. He watched as Clemente read down page twenty-two. The next page was the important page. The one with Brasselli's note on line ten.

Clemente turned to the next page. He began to read. Kent's heart accelerated.

Then suddenly Clemente frowned. He muttered something and turned the page, then turned back again to the previous page. He looked up.

"Is something wrong?" Kent asked. He wasn't looking at Christina, but he could feel her listening.

Tracy looked up, her hazel eyes curious.

Lisa stopped in the midst of collating some copies.

The room settled into quiet.

Then Clemente, dark eyes clouded, said, "There seems to be a page missing here."

"A page missing..." Kent repeated. He frowned, too. "Let me see."

Clemente handed the notebook to him.

Kent looked down. On the left was page twenty-two. On the right was page twenty-five. Pages twenty-three and twenty-four were gone.

Brasselli's notation was gone.

Kent looked up. He met Clemente's gaze. Then he turned to Christina.

Her cool gray eyes held that same smug look. That look that said, Didn't I tell you everything was under control?

Chapter Fifteen

Although dozens of thoughts raced through Kent's mind, he kept his face and voice impassive and only mildly curious. "Hmm. That's funny. I never noticed a page missing. Well..." He shrugged nonchalantly. "You know how they put these bindings together...." He examined the binding of the notebook and saw it was loose. He handed the notebook back to Clemente. "It probably just fell out. We'll look for it."

Clemente's face could have been cast from stone as he leveled his gaze at Kent. Kent willed himself not to think about the importance of the missing page. Later. In the privacy of his office he would think about it. But not now.

Finally Clemente spoke. "See that you do look for it."

Somehow Kent got through the rest of the after-noon. He avoided Christina's eyes because now was not the time to confront her, either. But at five o'clock, when Clemente looked at his watch and suggested, "Why don't we finish this up tomorrow?" he breathed a sigh of relief.

Once the two lawyers were gone and Lisa had returned to her office, he stood and walked to where Christina still sat. "What's going on?" he demanded.

"About what?"

"Don't give me that innocent look. You know damned well about what!"

Christina smiled with her cat-that-ate-the-canary look firmly in place. "Don't get so excited, Kent. I told you. Everything's under control."

His eyes narrowed, and he fought to control his temper. "What happened to page twenty-three?"

"Who knows? Like you said, those bindings are awfully loose."

"Did Jamieson remove it? Or did you?"

"Why, Kent!" Her tone was all innocence. "Removing evidence is against the law, and you know it."

"Yes. I know it. And so does Ben Keating."

Now that smug look evaporated, and a hardness took its place. "Do you also know what happens to young associates who try to make trouble for senior partners?"

"Is that a threat?" he countered.

"If I were you, I'd think long and hard before I went to Ben Keating. Remember. It'll just be your word against Colin's word that there even *was* a page twenty-three in existence."

Kent remembered the copy of page twenty-three that was still jammed somewhere in his briefcase. The copy that Armand Brasselli had tried to keep. The copy that would prove someone in this firm had tampered with evidence.

The copy that he could show Ben Keating.

Allison left a message for Kent at three o'clock, but he never called her back. She tried calling his office again at five-thirty, thinking he might be working late. Sunny, as instructed, had set up an appointment to look at the house at eight o'clock. Allison hoped she wouldn't have to call Sunny back and cancel, but if she didn't reach Kent, she might have to.

At six o'clock the phone rang. It was Kent.

"Hi," he said.

She immediately knew something was wrong. "Hi."

"Are you busy right now?"

"No, I—"

"I'm coming over. I'll be there in half an hour."

Allison started to say something about her message and the appointment to see the house, but he hung up before she could. She stared at the phone, her heart beating faster. What was wrong? She paced around for the next twenty minutes. What had happened to make Kent sound so ominous, so abrupt? Had there been a confrontation at work?

By the time Kent arrived a little after six-thirty, Allison was nervously imagining all sorts of things. And the sight of him, face tight and drawn, didn't set her at ease, either.

"Where are the folks?" he asked as he walked in. He was still dressed in his suit, but he'd loosened his tie and had obviously been running his hands through his hair.

"They were going out for dinner."

"Where's the baby?"

"She's at my grandmother's. That's why I called you, Kent. I made an appointment—"

"Allison, something happened today."

Immediately she stopped talking. "Come into the living room."

She listened as he told her about Jackson Clemente and Tracy Higgins and what they were doing at Keating & Shaw. And when he got to the part about the missing notebook page, she gasped. "Oh, Kent!"

"Christina denied knowing anything about it. In fact, she reminded me that I would be committing career suicide to accuse a senior partner of tampering with evidence, especially when I had no proof at all."

"But didn't you tell me you'd copied that page?" She was sure he had when he'd told her about his interview with Armand Brasselli.

"Yes." His gaze met hers.

"Well, then . . . you *do* have proof. Kent, you have to go to Ben Keating. This is terrible!"

His eyes, usually so clear and blue, looked as if the sun had gone out of them as they looked at her. "I don't have proof."

"I don't understand. . . ."

He smiled without mirth. "The copy is gone."

"The copy is gone!"

"Yep. Vanished without a trace."

"Kent! They took it!"

"Very probably."

"Wh-where was it?"

"It had been in my briefcase."

"How could they have taken it from your briefcase?"

"Easy. I leave my briefcase laying around my office all the time. When I'm at lunch. When I walk down to the copy room. When I'm in someone else's office. Anyone could go into my office and take something out of my briefcase."

Allison was appalled by this turn of events, but a tiny part of her was actually rejoicing, for now Kent would have no choice. He would have to leave the firm. And then everything would be the way it was always meant to be. She waited for him to echo her thoughts.

Instead, he leaned back on the couch and closed his eyes. "Jesus, I'm tired," he said. "I sure could use something to drink."

Allison stared at him.

A few seconds later he opened his eyes. He frowned. "Okay, sorry, I'll get myself a drink." He started to get up.

"I'll get you a drink, Kent. That's not the problem."

"Then what is?"

"Are you just going to forget about what happened today?"

"I suppose you think I should charge into Keating's office and start throwing accusations around."

"Yes. Of course I do. Tell him what's happened. He can't ignore this, Kent! And if he does, quit! You don't want to work there if this is the kind of thing that happens."

He stiffened. "You make everything sound so easy. But you're not the one sitting in my chair. It's my career that's on the line. And I don't intend to jeopardize my entire future out of some misguided sense of honor. Remember, I'm taking on a lot of responsibilities soon. I'm going to have a wife and a child to support."

"You can't just drop this, Kent. We'll manage. I've got money. Kent, just think! You can open the storefront again."

"I'll never touch a penny of your money. I told you that four years ago and I still feel that way. And about the storefront. How many times do I have to tell you? I have no intention of opening the storefront again. That part of my life is over!"

"You can't mean that."

Abruptly he stood. His eyes were no longer clouded. Now they blazed with blue fire. "My mind is made up, Allison, so let's just drop it, okay? I'm staying with Keating & Shaw, and I'm keeping my mouth shut about this missing page. It has nothing to do with me."

"Nothing to do with you! It has everything to do with you!" A coldness settled around her heart as she slowly stood to face him. "What's happened to you, Kent?" she asked sadly. "I don't even know you anymore."

His jaw hardened. "What the hell do you expect from me, Allison? I'm doing the best that I can. Isn't my best good enough for you? Are we back to that again? I can't seem to please you, no matter what I do. You always want more than I'm capable of giving." He walked to the front window, then swung around to face her again. "Make up your mind. Either accept me as I am, or we break it off now. Permanently!"

If a heart could actually break, Allison was sure hers would be cracking the same way an eggshell cracks. She couldn't accept Kent on these terms. She couldn't. This wasn't the Kent she knew and loved. And unless that Kent returned, unless he was true to himself, there would be nothing for them to build a future on. "I'm sorry, Kent," she whispered. "I'm so sorry." Tears burned behind her eyelids, and she tried to keep them from falling as she tugged at the ring on her finger.

On legs that threatened to buckle, she walked the few feet separating them and handed him the ring. Her fingers shook as he slowly opened his hand, never breaking eye contact, to accept it.

She bit her bottom lip to still its trembling and felt the hot tears sliding down her cheeks.

He swallowed once. Then, face white, fists clenched, he turned and walked away from her.

When he opened the front door and walked out, letting the door close behind him, Allison sank to the floor and cried and cried until there were no tears left.

The next week was the worst week of Allison's life. Worse than the week after she'd broken her first engagement to Kent. Worse than the week she realized she didn't love Jean Luc and he didn't love her. Worse than the week when she'd been told about Marianne's illness. Worse because this time there was no hope at all.

Her beautiful, wonderful dream was over.

Kent was gone. The Kent she had loved for so long didn't exist anymore. And she was to blame. All of this, all his problems, all their problems, could have been avoided if she'd only been mature enough years ago to realize what she'd had.

She couldn't hide her unhappiness. Diana and her father realized immediately that something had happened. Even if they hadn't had the obvious clue of the missing ring, they'd have only had to take one look at her stricken face to know.

Two days after the breakup, her father said, "Come on. Let's go for a ride and talk."

It was tempting to dump everything on her father's shoulders, but Allison knew she had to stop doing that. She was an adult, and she needed to solve her own problems. So she answered regretfully, "No, Dad. I appreciate your concern, but this is something I have to work out for myself.''

After thinking about it, she called her grandmother Marlowe and asked her if she and Marianne could move into the guest house on their property. Her grandmother was delighted, and that night Lee and Diana helped her move.

Once Allison and Marianne were ensconced in the little house, she thought how ironic it was that she should end up here, where four years ago everything had begun. She and her father had occupied the guest house when they'd first returned to Houston from their long sojourn in Europe, and shortly thereafter she'd met Kent.

How things had changed. Four years ago she was a young, spoiled, self-centered girl. Now she was a woman, and she hoped she'd learned something.

That night, after Marianne was asleep, Allison sat in the living room and began to think.

For two days after Allison had broken their engagement, Kent had been numb. He went to work and he went home. But nothing really penetrated his numbness.

On the third day, after thinking and thinking about what had happened and everything that led up to it, Kent knew that he'd been kidding himself for a long time. Allison had been right. This time she'd been right. And maybe all along he'd known she was right but hadn't wanted to admit it.

Maybe you just wanted to punish her.

The thought chilled him. Was that it? Was that it all along? Had he been stubbornly clinging to his position because he didn't want to give Allison the satisfaction and forgiveness she'd asked for? Because he wanted her to continue feeling guilty over their first breakup?

Sighing, he got up and paced around his office. No matter what his reasons were or had been, one thing was clear. He had to talk to Ben Keating. He couldn't live with himself if he didn't at least make an attempt to right a wrong.

No matter *what* happened to his future with the firm.

"Oh, Allison, I'm so sorry about you and Kent," Marcy said. The two of them were sitting in the living room of the guest house, with Marianne lying on a quilt Allison had placed on the floor beside them. Sunlight streamed over her, and she kicked happily.

Allison nodded. She had calmed down somewhat since her confrontation with Kent. She still ached inside. She still cried sometimes. But she had been doing a lot of soul-searching since Kent walked out. Trying to think how to begin, she picked at a thread on the couch. "You know, Marce, I've been thinking."

Marcy's soft eyes watched her face intently.

Allison hesitated. She wanted to say this right, so that Marcy would understand, but it was difficult because she was only just beginning to understand everything herself. "Do you think that the reason I've been so obdurate about Kent leaving Keating & Shaw and reopening the storefront is that I've been looking for absolution?"

Marcy frowned. "Absolution?"

Allison nodded. "I know it sounds weird but yesterday...all of a sudden...it just came to me. Maybe in all this I've felt so guilty about what happened years ago that I've lost sight of what's really happening now. Maybe in some twisted way I felt that if only Kent would quit his job with Keating & Shaw and reopen the storefront, I would no longer have to bear the burden for what went wrong between us."

Marcy slowly shook her head up and down. "You know, you might have something there."

Allison bit her lip. "Oh, Marce. What have I done?"

Kent walked purposefully down the hall. Ben Keating's secretary looked up from her computer. "Hello, Mr. Sorensen."

"Is Mr. Keating in?"

"Yes, but he's busy right—"

"Is someone in with him?" Kent asked, too determined to get this over with to wait for her to finish her sentence.

"No, but...Mr. Sorensen! You can't just go in there!" She leaped up.

Kent ignored her, continuing to head straight for Keating's door. He knocked once, then opened the door into Keating's office. The older man, who had been dictating, stopped in midsentence and set down the mike. "Kent? What's the meaning of this?"

Kent shut the door and walked straight to the desk. He didn't sit down. "I don't know if you're aware of this, sir, but Jackson Clemente and Tracy Higgins were here the other day to examine the documents on the Wilder case."

"Yes, I know—"

"Do you also know that while looking through the R & D notebooks, Clemente discovered a page missing from one of them?" Kent paused for one heartbeat. "The page containing the notation by Armand Brasselli? The notation I questioned?"

Keating frowned. His eyes darkened. He pursed his lips, his frown deepening. "No," he said slowly. "No, I wasn't aware of that."

"Someone in this firm removed that page, Mr. Keating. Someone who didn't want Clemente or Higgins to see it."

"That's a very serious accusation, Kent."

"I know that, sir. And I don't make it lightly. Believe me, I don't."

"Tampering with evidence is a crime," Keating said, voice soft, as if he were thinking aloud. He turned his chair slightly and stared off into space.

"Yes, it is."

Silence pulsed around them as Keating continued to frown. Kent could almost hear the wheels turning in the older man's head. After a long moment Keating cleared his throat and looked back up at Kent. "Sit down, Kent," he said.

Kent sat.

Keating picked up his phone. "Ginny, call Colin Jamieson and ask him to come to my office, please." He paused a moment. "Yes, now."

While they waited, neither man said anything. Keating seemed lost in thought, and Kent looked out the window. The only noises in the room were the ticking of the grandfather clock standing in one corner of Keating's office and the muffled ring of telephones outside the closed door. Outside the wall of windows behind Keating's desk, large white cumulus clouds floated by.

Finally there was a tap on the door. Kent tensed.

"Come in," Keating said.

Colin Jamieson, looking dapper and confident in a dark pin-striped suit paired with a teal green tie, walked in. He frowned when he spied Kent. "What's up, Ben?" he asked.

"Come on in, Colin, and close the door."

Jamieson did as instructed, then walked to the desk.

"Sit down, Colin. Kent has told me something that disturbs me."

"Oh? And what might that be?"

Kent marveled at the man's acting ability. Jamieson had to know what was coming, yet he managed to look innocent, as well as sound justifiably arrogant.

"Kent tells me that a page is missing from one of the R & D notebooks in the Wilder case. Did you know about this?"

Jamieson shrugged. "Christina Sargent mentioned something about it." He gave Keating an inscrutable look. "Something about the binding being loose, I think. It's not important."

Keating's gaze darted to Kent. "You didn't say anything about a loose binding. You said someone had removed the page."

"Someone *did* remove the page," Kent said.

"Now, wait a minute—" Jamieson said.

Ben Keating interrupted him. "Colin, hold on. Let me handle this, please."

Jamieson subsided, but not before shooting Kent a look that said Kent was going to pay for this.

"Kent," Keating said, "do you have any proof at all of this claim of yours?"

"No, Ben, I don't." Kent purposely used Keating's first name. "But Jamieson knows, and I know, and Christina knows, and I think you know that it's just too much of a coincidence that the one page that might contain something incriminating—something that could shoot holes into our defense—just happens to disappear before anyone but us has had a chance to see it.''

"Now see here," Jamieson sputtered.

Kent kept talking. ''If that's all that had happened, I might think it was an accident, that the binding really was loose. But that's not all.''

"What do you mean?" Keating asked.

"Yes, what do you mean?" Jamieson echoed, his tone belligerent.

"Two things. When I first mentioned this notation, Jamieson lied to me. He told me the plaintiff's attorneys had already looked at the R & D notebooks and saw nothing to question. They hadn't. And..." He paused. "And I made a copy of that page," Kent added softly.

Keating raised his eyebrows.

Jamieson's lips tightened, but he said nothing.

"And someone stole the copy out of my briefcase," Kent finished.

Keating stared at him, then slowly swiveled his gaze to Jamieson, who nonchalantly inspected his nails. "Do you know anything about this, Colin?" Keating asked.

Jamieson looked up. "Absolutely not. And I resent being called a liar. I never said the opposition had already looked at those notebooks."

Kent couldn't believe how the man could lie. Just sit there and lie with a straight face. He wondered if Ben Keating believed him. He wondered if any punishment would be doled out. He doubted it. Colin Jamieson was a senior partner with the firm. There was no proof of wrongdoing. It was only Kent's word, after all. The word of a young associate with no track record against that of a senior partner with a long history with the firm.

Kent stood. Both Keating and Jamieson looked up. The grandfather clock continued to tick. The clouds outside continued to sail by. Life continued to move on.

Kent took a deep breath. Suddenly he felt freer than he'd felt in a long time. He ignored Jamieson and addressed himself to Keating. "Ben, I don't know what you're going to do about this. I suspect nothing, but that's your problem, not mine. Personally I have no interest in being affiliated with a firm that condones this kind of thing. Effective immediately, I resign. I'll have an official letter of resignation on your secretary's desk before I leave today."

And then, knowing that he'd done the right thing, he turned and walked out.

He didn't look back.

After Marcy left, Allison decided that the only way she would ever know if there was still hope for her and Kent was to make the first move.

She picked Marianne up, grabbed her diaper bag and carried her to the main house. When her grandmother answered the door, Allison said, "Gran, I have two favors to ask."

"What are they, honey?" Jinx smiled, her green eyes welcoming.

"Will you watch Marianne for a couple of hours?"

"Of course." Jinx held out her arms. "Come here, sweetheart. Your great-grandma loves to watch you!" Marianne chortled as Jinx took her and held her close.

"And Gran? Do you think I could use your car?"

Kent stared at Lee. "When did she move out?"

"Yesterday."

"She's staying at the guest house again?"

Lee's eyes, which were so much like Allison's, held a cautious expression. "Yes."

"Thanks." Kent dashed back to his car, got in and started the engine. He pointed the Corvette in the direction of the Marlowe property.

Allison drove slowly down her grandparents' street. Maybe she should have called Kent first.

No. She would drive to his condo, and she would wait there until he came home.

When she got to the end of the street, the light was red, so she stopped. Out of the corner of her eye, she saw the white Corvette turn onto the street, and as it drew abreast of her, she recognized Kent.

At the same moment he looked her way.

His eyes widened.

Her heart stopped.

What was he doing here? Her stupid heart began to beat again. *Thump, thump, thump.* She stared at him.

He rolled his window down.

After a moment she rolled hers down.

"I was on my way to see you," he said.

Oh, his eyes were so blue! And she was so happy to see him! "I—I was on my way to see you."

"You were?" His eyes lit up, and he grinned.

Allison wanted to cry. She loved his smile so. She loved him so.

A car horn blared, and they both jumped. Kent laughed sheepishly as he realized he was blocking the road. "Turn around," he said. "I'll meet you at your grandmother's house." And with another grin, he took off down the street.

Heart still beating like a tom-tom, Allison backed up and turned her grandmother's Cadillac around. Hardly daring to hope, she pulled into the driveway and around to the back of the house where Kent had already parked his Corvette.

Suddenly afraid, she slowly got out of the car. Kent walked toward her, looking wonderful in baggy white cotton pants and a fire-engine red T-shirt with the University of Houston logo on it.

"Kent—"

"Allison—"

They both spoke at once, then they both fell silent again. Allison knew everything she was feeling must be right there in her eyes for all the world to see. There was so much she wanted to say. But she felt tongue-tied. And afraid.

Finally Kent stirred. He reached for her arm, and his touch sent tingles through her. "Let's go inside," he said, leading her toward the guest house.

As soon as the door closed behind them, Kent turned her to face him. Allison's heart thudded like a mad thing. "Allison, I have so much to tell you, I don't know where to start." Then he laughed. "Oh, hell, I'll start with the most important thing. I love you." He touched her cheek, and she closed her eyes for just a moment, reveling in the warmth of his hand against her skin. When she opened her eyes again, he smiled gently. "Two more things. I'm sorry. And I quit my job."

She could only stare at him. He'd quit his job. What did this mean?

"I was wrong and you were right," he said.

She finally found her voice. "No, no. I wasn't right. I only just realized it today. I was wrong to try to tell you what to do. Did you really quit your job?"

"Yes."

She swallowed hard. Maybe after all things would work out. "Do you really love me?" she whispered.

"I love you with all my heart."

"Oh, Kent. I love you, too."

And then as he opened his arms and she walked into them, he kissed her. And the kiss was like fireworks and bells ringing and love songs playing and all the romantic movies she'd ever seen. She kissed him back, touching her tongue to his, letting him sweep her away into that fairy-tale world where the most wonderful dreams really do come true.

A long time later, as they sat side by side on the sofa, Allison said, "Tell me what happened."

And so he did. And she marveled at his courage, because she knew it had taken a lot of courage to stand up for what he knew was right.

"I finally realized that if I stayed at Keating & Shaw, if I spent years defending clients like Emmett Wilder and working with people like Colin Jamieson, I'd slowly become one of them. And nothing—not money, not financial security, not a partnership with Keating & Shaw—is worth sacrificing my integrity and self-respect," he said.

Allison held his hand tighter.

"And I finally realized," she said, "that the only reason I was so dead set on you going back to the storefront was that I didn't want to feel it was my fault that your dream didn't work out." She looked up at his dear face. "Kent, I don't care what you do for a living. Go to work for another firm, go back to a storefront practice, even go back to Keating & Shaw. It's your decision, and I'm behind you all the way."

He smiled down at her, and then they kissed again.

Later he said, "I'm going to talk to Joel and Michael. Joel's been unhappy with his firm, and Michael would love to go into a partnership with us. How does that sound to you? Berry, Bartlett and Sorensen, attorneys-at-law?"

"Oh, Kent! That sounds wonderful!" Allison's heart felt too full. She wasn't sure she could handle this much happiness.

"We might not make a lot of money at first," Kent warned.

"That doesn't matter."

"But I might consider a loan from you...."

"Kent! Would you?" Maybe that house was still available. She would call Sunny tonight. She just knew Kent would love the house.

"And just to make you happy," he said, a twinkle in his eyes, "we'll devote part of our business to *pro bono* work. How does that sound?"

She grinned. "Yolanda?"

He gave her a long-suffering look. "You never give up, do you?"

Her grin widened.

"All right. I'll even take on Yolanda's case if she needs me." Then he kissed her ear, and she shivered. "Boy, woman," he whispered, "you certainly drive a hard bargain!"

This time, when Kent pulled the ring out of his pocket and placed it on her finger, Allison knew it would stay there forever.

Because after all, according to all the experts, the third time is a charm.

Epilogue

From the pages of the *Houston Herald*

AROUND HOUSTON
by B. J. Barrette

Once again the Sorensens and Gabriels have been united. This time the wedding that took place was the one scheduled for four years ago! Yes, Lee Gabriel's daughter, Allison Gabriel Fornier, and Diana Sorensen Gabriel's son, Kent William Sorensen, were finally united in marriage. The candlelight ceremony at St. John's was perfect in every way, down to the presence of the new Mrs. Sorensen's infant daughter, Marianne, who looked enchanting in a pink-satin-and-lace dress with matching shoes and hat.

The bride wore her maternal grandmother's—our own dear Jinx Marlowe's—antique satin wedding dress. Her two attendants, Marcy Bartlett and Gail Berry, wore wine silk dresses and carried yellow roses. All flowers were provided by Posey's Posies. Both the bride's sumptuous veil and her attendants' dresses were designed by our town's Alaina, who sells her much-sought-after finery through her West University boutique.

The groom, resplendent in black tails, was attended by his two partners in the newly formed law firm of Berry, Bartlett and Sorensen. Both Joel Bartlett, husband to Marcy, and Michael Berry, spouse of Gail, looked handsome and dignified and performed their duties masterfully.

The bride's father and the groom's mother held hands throughout the ceremony, and my spies tell me that the cool Diana actually shed a few tears! You read it here first!

Four hundred guests attended the reception at the country club, and you have it straight from me—the food, wine and music were heavenly. I can't remember when I've had such a good time.

The new Mr. and Mrs. Sorensen, after a wedding trip to Vancouver, will move into their newly purchased home in West University. They will be a welcome addition to the Houston social scene, and you'll probably read their names here in my column on a regular basis.

* * * * *

TAKE A WALK ON THE
DARK SIDE OF LOVE WITH

October is the shivery season, when chill winds blow and shadows walk the night. Come along with us into a haunting world where love and danger go hand in hand, where passions will thrill you and dangers will chill you. Silhouette's second annual collection from the dark side of love brings you three perfectly haunting tales from three of our most bewitching authors:

Kathleen Korbel
Carla Cassidy
Lori Herter

Haunting a store near you this October.

Only from 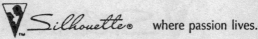 where passion lives.

SHAD93

Silhouette

SPECIAL EDITION™

Coming in
October,
the third book in
Debbie
Macomber's

*From this
day
forward*

MARRIAGE WANTED

Dash Davenport didn't marry Savannah Charles for love, only convenience.
As a divorce attorney, he knew marriage was a mistake. But as a man, Dash
couldn't resist Savannah's charms. It seemed Savannah knew all the makings
of a happily-ever-after. And it wasn't long after saying "I do" that Dash
started thinking about forever....

FROM THIS DAY FORWARD—Three couples marry first and
find love later in this heartwarming trilogy.

Only from Silhouette Special Edition.

Silhouette Books has done it again!

Opening night in October has never been as exciting! Come watch as the curtain rises and romance flourishes when the stars of tomorrow make their debuts today!

Revel in Jodi O'Donnell's STILL SWEET ON HIM—
Silhouette Romance #969
…as Callie Farrell's renovation of the family homestead leads her straight into the arms of teenage crush Drew Barnett!

Tingle with Carol Devine's BEAUTY AND THE BEASTMASTER—
Silhouette Desire #816
…as legal eagle Amanda Tarkington is carried off by wrestler Bram Masterson!

Thrill to Elyn Day's A BED OF ROSES—
Silhouette Special Edition #846
…as Dana Whitaker's body and soul are healed by sexy physical therapist Michael Gordon!

Believe when Kylie Brant's McLAIN'S LAW —
Silhouette Intimate Moments #528
…takes you into detective Connor McLain's life as he falls for psychic—and suspect—Michele Easton!

Catch the classics of tomorrow—*premiering* today—
only from ♥ *Silhouette*

PREM

**And now for
something completely different
from Silhouette....**

Every once in a while, Silhouette brings you a
book that is truly unique and innovative, taking
you into the world of paranormal happenings.
And now these stories will carry our special
"Spellbound" flash, letting you know that you're
in for a truly exciting reading experience!

In October, look for *McLain's Law* (IM #528)
by Kylie Brant

Lieutenant Detective Connor McLain believes
only in what he can see—until Michele Easton's
haunting visions help him solve a case...and her
love opens his heart!

McLain's Law is also the Intimate Moments
"Premiere" title, introducing you to a debut
author, sure to be the star of tomorrow!

Available in October...only from
Silhouette Intimate Moments

SPELL1

SILHOUETTE.... Where Passion Lives

Don't miss these Silhouette favorites by some of our most popular authors!
And now, you can receive a discount by ordering two or more titles!

Silhouette Desire®

#05751	THE MAN WITH THE MIDNIGHT EYES BJ James	$2.89 ☐
#05763	THE COWBOY Cait London	$2.89 ☐
#05774	TENNESSEE WALTZ Jackie Merritt	$2.89 ☐
#05779	THE RANCHER AND THE RUNAWAY BRIDE Joan Johnston	$2.89 ☐

Silhouette Intimate Moments®

#07417	WOLF AND THE ANGEL Kathleen Creighton	$3.29 ☐
#07480	DIAMOND WILLOW Kathleen Eagle	$3.39 ☐
#07486	MEMORIES OF LAURA Marilyn Pappano	$3.39 ☐
#07493	QUINN EISLEY'S WAR Patricia Gardner Evans	$3.39 ☐

Silhouette Shadows®

#27003	STRANGER IN THE MIST Lee Karr	$3.50 ☐
#27007	FLASHBACK Terri Herrington	$3.50 ☐
#27009	BREAK THE NIGHT Anne Stuart	$3.50 ☐
#27012	DARK ENCHANTMENT Jane Toombs	$3.50 ☐

Silhouette Special Edition®

#09754	THERE AND NOW Linda Lael Miller	$3.39 ☐
#09770	FATHER: UNKNOWN Andrea Edwards	$3.39 ☐
#09791	THE CAT THAT LIVED ON PARK AVENUE Tracy Sinclair	$3.39 ☐
#09811	HE'S THE RICH BOY Lisa Jackson	$3.39 ☐

Silhouette Romance®

#08893	LETTERS FROM HOME Toni Collins	$2.69 ☐
#08915	NEW YEAR'S BABY Stella Bagwell	$2.69 ☐
#08927	THE PURSUIT OF HAPPINESS Anne Peters	$2.69 ☐
#08952	INSTANT FATHER Lucy Gordon	$2.75 ☐

	AMOUNT	$ _____
DEDUCT:	10% DISCOUNT FOR 2+ BOOKS	$ _____
	POSTAGE & HANDLING	$ _____
	($1.00 for one book, 50¢ for each additional)	
	APPLICABLE TAXES*	$ _____
	TOTAL PAYABLE	$ _____
	(check or money order—please do not send cash)	

To order, complete this form and send it, along with a check or money order for the total above, payable to Silhouette Books, to: *In the U.S.*: 3010 Walden Avenue, P.O. Box 9077, Buffalo, NY 14269-9077; *In Canada*: P.O. Box 636, Fort Erie, Ontario, L2A 5X3.

Name: _____

Address: _____ City: _____

State/Prov.: _____ Zip/Postal Code: _____

*New York residents remit applicable sales taxes.
Canadian residents remit applicable GST and provincial taxes.

SBACK-OD

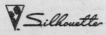